Unquiet Spirit

By the same author

Tripletree
The Nature of Rare Things

Unquiet Spirit

Derek Wilson

Constable • London

Constable & Robinson Ltd
3 The Lanchesters
162 Fulham Palace Road
London W6 9ER
www.constablerobinson.com

First published by Constable,
an imprint of Constable & Robinson Ltd 2006

A copy of the British Library Cataloguing in
Publication Data is available from the British Library

ISBN-13: 978-1-84529-346-8
ISBN-10: 1-84529-346-0

Printed and bound in the EU

Prelude: Christmas is Coming

It was the perfect night for a ghost hunt. So, at least, it might have seemed to devotees of old Hammer horror movies and the psycho-dramas of Hollywood. True, there was no thunder and lightning but rain fell in unremitting cascades from a hearse-black sky and a December wind thrashed it about Cambridge's ancient courts and buildings. The last frenzied Christmas shoppers had long since deserted the neon-lit entreaties of Lion Yard and the Grafton Centre. Few vehicles roamed the streets of a city which found itself in that hiatus period when preparations for the mid-winter fest had not quite ended and the partying had not quite begun.

Midway along Jesus Lane the massive Gothic portal of St Thomas's College was firmly shut. Inside, the lamp standards at each corner of Chapel Court illuminated the silver shoals of rain that plashed past almost horizontally. A few lighted windows indicated the presence of fellows and senior members in residence. Otherwise all was darkness.

There were no lights on F staircase but it was inhabited. Its cramped first-floor landing was occupied by three people who held torches and communicated in brief, hushed sentences. Andy Rowsell hunched over the equipment he had set up in the open doorway of the college servants' room and muttered to himself as he scrutinized the array of computer screens.

'Any readings yet, Andy?' Cynthia – Little Cynth, as most people knew her – called out for the third time from where she sat, huddled inside her heavy topcoat, at the top of the staircase which curled down to the ground floor.

For the third time, Andy ignored the question.

The chilled silence returned, somehow intensified by the relentless pattering of rain on the college servants' room window. Then, close by, the chapel clock chimed once.

'Eleven thirty.' Jenny Collard detached herself from the door against which she had been leaning, hands thrust deep into the pockets of her anorak. 'Cynth, perhaps you'd like to take a look upstairs.'

Before the teenager could respond, Andy said, 'No way! No bloody way! She'll go blundering into my camera, recorders and sensors. It took me ages to get them set up in exactly the right places.'

Jenny shone her torch in Cynthia's direction. With several hours' vigil to go it was essential for the leader to assert her authority. 'I'm sure she'll be careful, won't you, Cynth?'

By way of response Andy grunted, then added, 'Well, you'd better go, too. Show her where everything is. Anyway, she's probably too scared to go by herself up the haunted stairs. Whooo!' He took two paces across the narrow landing, waving his hands at Cynthia, who jumped up and shrank back against the wall.

'Andy, shut up!' Jenny flashed her torch full in his face. 'This is a serious experiment, not some adolescent lark!'

'Ooh, sorry, Miss. Shall I go and stand in the corner?' He turned back to his equipment.

Jenny shrugged and not for the first time wondered why Andy had volunteered his services to the Psychic Investigation Unit. Not that one could be choosy. The shoestring organization needed all the help it could get. The young PhD student was certainly an expert on the technical aspects of a vigil. Jenny glanced approvingly at the cables, neatly taped together, snaking their way up the staircase. It would just make life so much easier if he could avoid getting everyone's back up. She tugged the woolly hat further

6

down over her ears. 'Come on, then, Cynth,' she said. 'Let's see if we can see anything happening up there.'

She led the way into the blackness of the upper staircase. Cynthia followed very close behind, nervously watching where she put her feet.

A sudden crash shattered the silence.

Cynthia let out a squeak. She grabbed at Jenny's coat to stop herself falling back.

For several seconds the three investigators froze. Then there came the sound of heavy footfalls on the lower staircase. Someone had come in from the courtyard, banging the door behind them.

The figure that emerged was a bulky man in his sixties holding before him a dripping umbrella which he proceeded to shake vigorously as he stepped on to the landing.

'Aha,' the newcomer announced peering through the gloom. 'The witching hour approaches. Thought it was high time I showed up. Wouldn't want to miss the fun when the spooks appear.'

Jenny hoped her involuntary grimace did not show. 'Good evening, Professor. Good of you to join us. May I introduce my colleagues. This is I think you know, Cynthia Fell and Andrew Rowsell? This is Professor Hockridge, fellow of St Thomas's. I mentioned that he'd probably be joining us.'

'No "probably" about it, Miss Collard. I insisted. When my esteemed colleagues agreed to all this hocus-pocus,' he waved a hand in the direction of Andy's consoles, 'I told them there would have to be an official college presence. I'm it.'

'I take it you think this is all a waste of time,' Andy responded. Jenny could sense his suppressed hostility.

The half-light sculpted the professor's flaccid features into harsh lines and gave his superior smile the appearance of a melodramatic leer. 'My dear young man, I'm sure you and your friends believe in what you're doing. I'm equally sure that you mean well. But if ever I was persuaded to take this psychic stuff seriously – well, I'd have to unlearn over forty years of scientific training. We live in a physical universe and everything in it is governed by physical laws. The fact that we don't yet understand how all those laws work is no reason to fill in the gaps with medieval super-stition.'

Under his breath Andy muttered something that sounded to Jenny like 'patronizing bastard'. Aloud he said, 'Wouldn't you agree that a scientist's worst enemy is a closed mind?'

'Certainly.'

'Good, because what we're engaged in here is a scientific experiment. We've got up-to-date equipment – surveillance cameras, digital still cameras, microphones, CD recording gear, passive infra-red detectors, thermometers and baro-meters, all linked into a computer. If anything happens up there,' Andy nodded towards the staircase, 'which can't yet be explained by your physical laws, it'll be recorded. We'll have evidence – data we can analyse. Nothing very medieval about that.'

Hockridge gave a grunt by way of reply, then turned his back on Andy. 'Well, let's see if we can't summon up this spectre of yours.'

He took a pace across the landing. Andy quickly followed and laid a restraining hand on his shoulder. 'For God's sake watch where you're going. All this stuff's expensive.'

The professor did not turn. 'I have my own torch here. You needn't be worried that I'll break your precious toys.' He clicked on his torch and a powerful beam splashed the curving stairs with light. Purposefully he began to climb. Andy glared after him.

'Sorry about this, Andy,' Jenny said, following Hockridge's progress up the stairs. 'You know we had to agree to let the professor come. Hopefully he'll have a nose round then leave us in . . .'

'What the . . . Aagh!'

The scream came from the upper staircase.

The investigators stared at the bend of the stairs round which Hockridge had just disappeared.

They saw him fall back, arms flailing. They heard the bony crack as his head struck one of the stone steps. Then the heavy body half-rolled, half-slithered till it lay sprawled at their feet.

For a moment the three of them stared down at the motionless figure. It was Andy who recovered first. He knelt beside the recumbent form and flashed a torch in his face. 'Out cold,' he muttered. 'See what you can do for him, Jenny. Cynth, you'd better come with me. Let's find out what frightened our fat friend.'

He set off up the stairs with the visibly trembling Cynthia almost treading on his heels.

Jenny bent over the professor who had fallen, face upwards. Uncertain what to do, she tried shaking his shoulder. 'Professor! Professor Hockridge! Are you OK?' Then she noticed the blood forming a pool around his head. 'Damn! Damn! Damn!' Desperately she tried to remember the elementary first aid she had once learned. What was she supposed to do? Loosen his clothing? She scrabbled at his tie and collar. 'Come *on*! Wake up!' she muttered. Then she brought her face close to the upturned face.

The rain had eased. The silence was intense.

After several seconds Jenny stood up. She felt for the wall and leaned against it for support. Words came eventually in short gasps. 'Andy ... I think ... I think he isn't ... breathing.'

''Twas the Night Before Christmas'

The Vice-Chancellor's Christmas Eve parties are highlights of the Cambridge social calendar and invitations are greatly prized by members of town and gown. The office of Vice-Chancellor is held in rotation by heads of colleges, and this provides scope for a certain amount of individuality in the drawing up of guest lists but protocol dictates that the majority of invitees will be masters, faculty heads, civic dignitaries and their wives. Dr Nathaniel Gye, lecturer in parapsychology and fellow of Beaufort College, was therefore flattered and surprised to receive an invitation. He was also intrigued to know why the embossed, gilt-edged card had arrived only three days before the event.

'I still reckon we were only invited to make up numbers,' Kathryn Gye said as they walked the short distance along Trumpington Street from Beaufort to the Fitzwilliam Museum, the venue for this year's event. Even after eight years of living in Britain her voice had not lost its soft, American drawl.

'Very possibly,' Nat shrugged, 'but it's not the sort of chance you turn down.'

'Well, promise me we won't stay too long. I've still got a hell of a lot of wrapping to do.'

'You and me both,' Nat agreed. 'Still, your folks won't be sorry if we don't hurry back. They've been longing to spend some time alone with the boys ever since they flew in from

11

Pittsburgh. Your mother's eyes positively lit up when I said we'd leave them to put Ed and Jerry to bed.'

They climbed the steps to the Fitzwilliam's Corinthian portico, deposited their topcoats and joined the queue moving up the staircase to be presented to their host and hostess.

'Nine thirty,' Kathryn whispered in her husband's ear. 'Not a minute longer.'

'OK.' Nat grinned and stooped forward to mutter conspiratorially, 'Let's synchronize watches.'

Kathryn grimaced. 'I know you too well, Nat Gye. It'll be, "Hang on a moment, Darling. There's one more person I must have a word with," and you'll disappear back into the mêlée for half an hour.'

'I promise. Nine thirty and we're away.'

A couple of hours later, when Nat checked his watch he complimented himself for keeping his word. It was eighteen minutes past nine and he reckoned he had done his social duty. He had chatted with everyone he wanted to chat with and several that he did not particularly want to chat with. He had done the circuit of the first-floor galleries under the gaze of seventeenth- and eighteenth-century portraits, drunk three glasses of a more-than-passable Chablis and eaten his quota of *bouchées*.

He was just about to go in search of Kathryn when someone behind him said, 'Dr Gye, isn't it?'

Nat turned and saw a small, rotund figure with silvery-grey hair brushed back from a lined forehead. Nat knew at once that he ought to be able to put a name to the face. The man, immaculate in hand-sewn, pinstriped worsted, had the air of someone who expected to be recognized. Nat cudgelled his memory as he shook the outstretched hand.

After a few embarrassed seconds, the stranger came to his rescue. 'Joseph Zuylestein. How do you do, Dr Gye.'

'Sir Joseph, delighted to meet you.' Recollection at last kicked in: Sir Joseph Zuylestein, retired international banker, recently installed as the new Master of St Thomas's. 'Are you settling well in Cambridge?'

The little man made a non-committal noise and Nat noticed the anxiety in his eyes and the nervous flapping of his hands.

Zuylestein said, 'Dr Gye, can you spare me a few minutes?'

Nat resisted the temptation to glance at his watch. 'Of course, but . . .'

'Good, good. Let's . . . er . . . Please.' He turned abruptly and weaved his way to a door in a corner of the gallery. He ushered Nat into what proved to be a small unoccupied office and closed the door behind him. 'Won't you, please . . .' He motioned Nat to a chair but remained standing himself.

Several seconds of awkward silence followed before Zuylestein said, 'I realize this must seem absurdly cloak and dagger but I'm afraid I've been guilty of a little deception. I persuaded the Vice-Chancellor to invite you because I wanted very much – very much indeed – to meet you confidentially.'

'Surely, Sir Joseph, a simple telephone call . . .'

The other man shook his head energetically. 'No, no, it isn't possible to arrange things in the conventional way. Please, bear with me a moment and I'll explain.'

'Well, Sir Joseph, as it happens I am in something of a hurry. We have people staying for Christmas and my wife and I . . .'

'Of course, of course. I mustn't trespass on your family celebration.' He drew a long white envelope from an inside pocket. 'I've written down the salient facts and I'll let you have this if you decide you can help us. First I had to meet you – away from the public gaze – to see if I could persuade you to at least consider coming to our aid.'

He paused and seemed again to be floundering for words. 'You might already have guessed what this is about,' he ventured eventually.

'Professor Hockridge's death? I was sorry to hear . . .'

'Exactly so, Dr Gye, exactly so. "The St Thomas's ghost strikes again." The press have had a field day over this untimely accident. The college has been besieged . . .

besieged. First it was just the *Cambridge Evening Star*. Then the television people turned up with their cameras bombarding the porters' lodge. Now the national tabloids have got on the track of a supposedly sensational story. We've had media people all over the place. Perhaps you begin to understand the need for this somewhat theatrical tête-à-tête. If I'd been seen to be consulting Cambridge's most celebrated expert on the ... er ... supernatural ... Well, you can imagine tomorrow's headlines: "TV ghost hunter to lay St Tom's spook."'

'Having one's face on television can certainly be a problem. But I can't really see why you want to "consult" me, as you say. As I understand it, Professor Hockridge suffered a heart attack while assisting in an experiment being carried out by the Psychic Investigation Unit. The circumstances were certainly bizarre but wouldn't the best policy be simply to ignore the media circus? By the time Christmas is over they'll have moved on to pastures new. It'll be a nine-days wonder.'

'Would that that were true, Dr Gye. Would that that were true. Jeremy's – Professor Hockridge's – death is just the latest in a string of incidents stretching back long before I came to St Thomas's. You doubtless know the bare details.'

Nat nodded. 'One of the St Tom's undergrads died of a drug overdose some ten years ago. A tragic business but sadly not all that uncommon. Since then there have been occasional unexplained disturbances in his rooms.'

'Substantially correct. The boy's name was Paul Sutton, a third-year student living in F5. After his death, the room wasn't exactly popular with junior members. You know how superstitions can develop. There were supposed manifestations. Of course, all this is what I've gleaned from fellows and college staff – members and visitors began claiming to hear noises and see ghostly shapes. It proved difficult to find anyone willing to take up residence there.'

'I've heard some of the stories.' Nat was becoming intrigued despite himself.

'Exactly! That's just the point. Everyone heard the stories – and the inevitable exaggerations of the stories. And they did no good for the college's image. But how to stop them? In my predecessor's day there were frequent, sometimes heated arguments among the fellows. Suggested solutions varied from exorcism to psychic investigations. Eventually – characteristically perhaps – the decision was taken to do . . . nothing.' Zuylestein's lips curled in disdain. 'Mental paralysis – the curse of academe! F5 was closed. It's now a lumber room. Everyone hoped the problem would go away. Pah! Ostriches and sand come to mind.'

'And you reversed this policy, Sir Joseph?'

Zuylestein allowed himself the faintest of smiles. 'There's no secret about my election as Master. My whole professional life has been in the world of finance and St Thomas's desperately needs money. The college decided it was high time to make friends of unrighteous mammon. It's up to me to deliver the goods and I can do so. I have the contacts which could, potentially, unlock millions in benefaction.'

'But not if St Thomas's can't handle a situation which makes it look slightly ridiculous?'

Sir Joseph turned to stare out of the window at the lights on the far side of Coe Fen. 'I can't, of course, comment on delicate negotiations in hand but what you say is substantially correct. We have strong competitors for the financial resources available. I was – still am – of the opinion that we should clear the matter up once and for all. I took the bull by the horns and persuaded the governing body to ask Jenny Collard and the PIU to do a proper scientific investigation. Jeremy Hockridge was violently opposed to the idea and he was followed by a sizeable faction. I got my motion through but Jeremy insisted on personally keeping a watching brief – with what turned out to be fatal results.'

'Very awkward for the college,' Nat said, 'but I'm afraid I don't see what I can do to help.'

'You have a reputation in these matters.'

15

Nat opened his mouth to respond but Zuylestein hurried on. 'No false modesty, please, Dr Gye. I've made careful enquiries, not least of your friend, Jenny Collard. We have to have a swift conclusion of this wretched business – swift and discreet. There's only one person I know of who can do it.'

Nat shook his head. 'I'm flattered, of course, Sir Joseph, but . . .'

Zuylestein brandished the envelope. 'I haven't told you everything. There have been certain other developments – unpleasant, even sinister developments – which I cannot divulge if you choose not to help us. I don't exaggerate when I say that they could prove absolutely disastrous for St Thomas's. I'm asking – begging if you like – for your assistance. I wouldn't dream of anything suggesting bribery but we would certainly demonstrate our appreciation for anything you could do for us.' He laid the envelope on the desk beside Nat's chair. 'If you decide to help you will find most of the material you need in there. If not I know I can count on you not to repeat anything of our conversation elsewhere.'

The moments of awkward silence that followed were broken by the chiming of an ornate marble clock which stood on a corner table.

'Oh my God!' Nat jumped up. 'Sir Joseph, I really must go. I'll think seriously about what you've said.'

He dashed to the door, fled through the gallery occupied now by only a few lingering guests and catering staff collecting up plates and glasses, and strode down the staircase towards the figure of Kathryn, standing in the foyer with a face like thunder. Only as he reached her, searching desperately for words of apology, did he realize that in his right hand he was clutching a long white envelope.

16

The Second Day of Christmas

'The best thing about Christmas is the day after.' Kathryn yawned, stretched and then nestled into the pillow.

Beside her, Nat echoed the yawn. He was lying in his dressing gown on top of the covers. 'Actually, it's the day after the day after. Look, the papers are here to prove it.' He rustled the copy of *The Times* that he was reading.

Kathryn groaned. 'Well, it just felt like it was going on for ever. Next year we'll book into a hotel and pay someone else to pamper us.'

'It was great having your parents here and they really enjoyed themselves.'

'Beats me where they get the energy from at their age. Playing party games into the small hours then up again early to set off on their lightning European tour. Paris today, then Vienna for New Year. It makes my head spin just thinking about it.'

'Ed and Jerry really loved the gear your folks gave them. When I went down to collect the paper just now they were already out in the garden doing pitching practice.'

Kathryn edged herself up to a sitting position. 'Well anything that prises them away from video games has to be a good thing. And the longer we can put off breakfast the better.' She rubbed her temples. 'My head's still throbbing from last night's party. Terry's fruit cup was lethal.'

'Would you like me to get you a coffee?'

'No, thanks.' She turned on to her side. 'Stop being so disgustingly energetic. Wake me up some time next year.'

17

Nat peered at her over the top of his reading glasses. 'We'll have to rejoin the land of the living soon. We promised to take the boys swimming.'

Kathryn groaned. 'Can't we put it off till tomorrow?'

'Yes, if you'll explain to them. Actually I have to go into Cambridge anyway. I must return that letter to St Tom's.'

'What!' Kathryn was suddenly awake and sitting up. 'Why do you want to do that?'

'Because I can't see that I can do anything to help them.'

'I thought you said taking the letter from Zuylestein meant that you were committed.'

'I know, but I've been thinking about it. I haven't read the letter, so if I return it unopened with a suitably apologetic note I shan't be morally bound to get involved.'

'But why don't you want to get involved? It's the sort of incident that's right up your street.'

Nat dropped the newspaper on the floor. 'I wish people would stop tell me that anything vaguely connected with the supernatural is "up my street".'

Kathryn frowned. 'OK, let me rephrase that. It sounds like an interesting case. You don't usually turn your back on unusual happenings like this one.'

Nat shrugged. 'What's interesting? A fat old don who notoriously abuses his body with brandy and general overindulgence falls down a stone staircase and has a heart attack. The police pathologist was satisfied that that was what happened. So, where's the story?'

'The story is in *why* he fell. What did he see that caused him to miss his footing?' Kathryn was glaring and Nat noticed that her cheeks were flushed.

'I don't know what he saw, what he thought he saw or whether he saw anything at all. Nor does anybody else. That's the point.'

'You've lost me.'

Nat gave a long-suffering sigh. 'I should have thought it was obvious. Whenever I investigate the supposed sighting of a supernatural phenomenon the first thing I do is talk to

18

the witnesses. I have to know whether any of them were psychologically "programmed" to have an unexplained experience; try to identify possible unconscious reactions; determine whether the subject is prone to unusual stress – you know the sort of thing. That's where I start. That's where any proper psychic investigation starts. Well, in this case there's only one witness and I can't very well interview him.'

'I thought Zuylestein said there were other confidential issues that hadn't come out so far.'

'Yes, well that's the crux of it. St Tom's has serious money problems. Everyone knows that.' Nat swung his legs over the edge of the bed. 'Zuylestein is looking round desperately for anyone who can pull their financial chestnuts out of the fire. I'm not the right guy for that sort of job.'

'But . . . Oh, you're impossible!' Kathryn looked daggers at him.

'Why? What have I done?'

'I'll bet if this story had been sent to you by one of your TV fans you'd be rushing to follow it up.'

Nat stared into the dressing table mirror and brushed his thinning hair. 'That's fair comment. I *am* chary of this St Tom's business. It's too close to home.'

He saw Kathryn's puzzled frown in reflection and went on. 'It's all this cloak and dagger stuff. I couldn't keep it up. People would know I was involved. Colleagues, not to mention my professor, would want to know what I was up to. I'd be hounded by the press. And if any confidential information leaked out, guess who'd get the blame. Anyway, why are you so keen for me to become Sir Joseph's whipping boy?'

Kathryn slipped out of bed and strode across to the bathroom. As the door closed behind her, she muttered, 'I read the letter.'

Minutes later, when she re-emerged, Nat was standing in the same place, scowling. 'Some kind of explanation might be in order,' he said, with what he considered to be masterly self-control.

With studied nonchalance Kathryn began extracting clothes from a drawer. 'I was damned cross when you kept me waiting after the Vice-Chancellor's party. Then you came bounding down the staircase, babbling something about a mysterious meeting with the Master of St Tom's and brandishing an envelope.' She pulled off her nightdress and turned towards him with a defiant stare. 'I was curious. I thought you owed me.'

'So you ripped open the envelope without bothering to say anything to me.'

Kathryn sat on the bed with her back to him as she wriggled into a pair of jeans. 'I didn't know you were desperate to keep it secret from me.'

'Oh, don't be silly!' Nat yanked open a wardrobe and began rummaging for his clothes. 'It's not a question of keeping anything from you. It's just that you've made things damned difficult for me with Zuylestein.'

'Perhaps if you'd bothered to tell me that you weren't going to take on this St Tom's problem . . .' Her voice was muffled as she pulled an Aran sweater over her head.

Nat grabbed a shirt from its hanger. 'Oh, of course, I should have realized that it was all my fault. Silly of me!'

'Now you're being childish!' Kathryn strode to the door. She turned briefly before leaving. 'You can't wear that shirt. It needs washing.'

After a frosty breakfast Nat went up to his study. He found the envelope and scrutinized it. It had obviously been opened neatly with a knife but there was no way of concealing the fact. He took out two thick sheets of college notepaper. He laid them on the desk without unfolding them. He stared at them. His hand hovered over the crisp, white stationery. He smoothed the pages out and saw the St Thomas's crest and, below it, several lines of tidy, very small handwriting. Then, with a sudden movement, he slipped the letter back into the envelope. He took a sheet of his own notepaper from a desk drawer and began to write. Choosing his words with great care he explained that though the master's letter had been opened by mistake, he was returning it unread. He wished Sir Joseph well in clearing up the business of the college 'ghost' but regretted that he felt unable to help. Then he sealed all the papers inside another envelope, marked it 'Sir Joseph Zuylestein – PRIVATE AND CONFIDENTIAL' and zipped it inside the bag in which he had already packed his swimming gear.

Kathryn had cried off the expedition to the pool, claiming that with everyone else out of the house she would be able to do some serious post-Christmas tidying up. Nat knew it was an excuse but declined to argue, even though their sons pulled faces and grumbled. After an energetic hour in the water the boys decided that they were so famished that only a burger would satisfy them. Nat resisted the demand for Big Macs and the argument continued all the way from the leisure centre and across Parker's Piece. Eventually Nat compromised by agreeing to Kentucky Fried Chicken. The three of them had just settled to their 'finger-licking' meal at a table in the window when a voice behind them said, 'Hello, Nat, I didn't know you were a KFC fan.'

Nat turned and saw a diminutive young woman with short dark hair crammed under a bright red bobblehat. 'Jenny, how nice.' He smiled, genuinely pleased to see his infectiously enthusiastic ex-doctoral student. 'Have you eaten? Come and join us.'

Jenny Collard plonked her carton on the table and perched beside Jerry. 'Hi, boys,' she said. 'Had a good Christmas?'

Ed and Jerry muttered something through mouthfuls of chips and were soon happily reminiscing about presents received and games played for Jenny's benefit. Eventually she glanced at Nat. 'And what about the harassed parents? How was it for you?'

'Harassed,' Nat replied with a laugh.

'And now, I suppose, you've left the little woman doing all the clearing up. Men!'

'Kathryn's choice entirely,' Nat protested.

21

Minutes of small talk followed before Jenny asked, wrinkling her freckled nose in a frown, 'By any chance, has the Master of St Tom's contacted you?'

'Yes, he invited me to a party last week – at your instigation, I gather.'

'Good . . . And?' She looked at him, head on one side, blue-grey eyes sparkling with curiosity.

'And what?'

'Oh, come on, Nat. Don't be infuriating. Old Sir Joe talked to you about the nasty business with Prof Hockridge, didn't he?'

'Yes, that must have been a nasty shock for you.'

'I've had better days. Hockridge was a pain in the arse. He didn't want our investigation and he was doing his level best to mess it up but . . .' Jenny waved a hand by way of finishing the sentence.

'What exactly happened? If you don't mind talking about it?'

'I don't mind. Quite the opposite. I'd probably have come to see you anyway, if I hadn't bumped into you like this.'

'Why?'

'I don't know, really.' She frowned distractedly and chewed a mouthful of chicken in silence. 'I'm sure that there's some evidence I'm missing. Naturally, I'd like to believe that the professor's fall was the result of some psychic phenomenon. Did he see something . . . or feel something? Was he pushed? It all happened so suddenly . . . And yet I have this nagging feeling that if only I could get every detail clear in my mind . . . Oh, I dunno.' She sighed her frustration.

His interest roused, Nat said, 'Try going through the events in order. That often helps.'

'I seem to have done very little else for the last couple of weeks. You know what it's like when you have a nagging problem in your head. It keeps popping up when you're trying to get on with other things.'

'OK, let me start you off. You took your PIU team to

St Tom's to investigate some manifestations in one of the student rooms.'

'It was pretty difficult right from the start. The fellows were embarrassed about inviting us there. They tried to swear us to complete secrecy. Well, you know how impossible that is. Any sniff of the supernatural and everyone gets curious. Still, we did our best. No one knew the date of our vigil except the handful of people who had to know. I'll swear nothing leaked out at our end. I'm sure the staircase and the rooms off it were empty when we got there. It was a vile night so there was hardly anyone around in the college. We helped Andy get his gear set up.'

'Andy?'

'Andy Rowsell. You haven't met him?'

Nat shook his head.

'Anorak with attitude! Technical whiz kid. Absolutely brilliant with computers and things but not so hot with human beings.'

'Who else was there?'

'Just Little Cynth – Cynthia Fell. Nice kid – in a cloying sort of way. Insecure and desperately eager to please. She's doing a psychology course at the local FE college. Nat, why is it that Psychology attracts so many inadequates and weirdos?'

'Most people think we're all nutters. Perhaps they're right. So, there were just the three of you?'

'Yes, I know the textbooks say there should be at least five – important to cross-check observations and responses and all that sort of thing – but you try rounding up volunteers to stand all night on a freezing cold staircase in the middle of winter. Actually there wouldn't have been much room for anyone else. We were pretty cramped on that little landing.'

'It was just the staircase you were examining, was it?'

Jenny pulled a face and shook her head. 'Thereby hangs a tale. The disturbances have been reported in the second-floor bedsit, F5, as well as the staircase. It was in F5 that poor Paul Sutton topped himself ten years ago.'

'I thought he was supposed to have died of a drug overdose.'

'Yeah, well that goes down as self-slaughter in my book. Stupid! Anyway, whatever happened happened in F5 but we weren't allowed to set up in there.'

'Why ever not?'

'The room's been shut up for some years. It's just used to store junk now. The bursar was one of the fellows who didn't approve of our being there and he said there was no way he was going to waste staff time having the room emptied for a bunch of what he called "cranky ghost-busters". The most he would do was leave the door un-locked for us. I looked in there when we arrived but it was piled high with chairs, tables and so on. Useless for us.'

'Sounds pretty unsatisfactory. What were you hoping to discover?'

'I've collected fifteen first-person statements from people who claim to have seen or heard something strange. All the usual sort of thing – footsteps, vague, insubstantial shapes. I hoped these would be repeated and we could catch some-thing on camera or mike.'

'No luck?'

'We never had a chance. We were all ready by about ten. Then, on the dot of eleven thirty, Old Hockridge came blundering in. He marched straight past us up the stairs. What happened next has been graphically described in the media.'

'Still, tell me in your own words.'

Jenny closed her eyes, revisiting the scene. 'Well, I watched him climb up towards the second landing. We all did. He'd just gone round the bend in the stairs when he let out this terrible scream . . . a sort of high-pitched, gurgling sound. It was hideous. I'll never forget it. Then he toppled over backwards and came crashing down, head first.' She paused to take a mouthful of coffee. 'He was lying right there at my feet. Of course, I bent down to see if he was badly hurt. It wasn't . . . very pleasant.'

'I'm sorry. It was silly of me to ask you to go through it all again.'

She shook her head emphatically. 'No, that's OK, Nat. I need to do it. I'm sure there's something not right, something I'm remembering wrong. I can see Hockridge's face quite vividly – sort of frozen in an expression of horror. I tried not to look at it as I fumbled around pretty ineffectually trying to do something for him. Then I realized his head was bleeding – quite profusely.'

Suddenly Nat noticed that Ed and Jerry were listening intently to Jenny's story. He pulled a fistful of loose change from his pocket. 'Here you are, boys. Go and get yourselves another Coke.'

Edmund looked up brightly. 'I'm OK, Dad, I don't need . . .'

Nat fixed his elder son with a stare. 'Then go and get an ice cream. Go on, both of you.'

With a grimace Ed slipped off his stool and his brother followed.

Jenny grinned. 'Sorry, I forgot how much kids take in. Anyway, there's not much more to tell. I realized the prof was probably dead and assumed he'd banged his head badly on the stone steps. It turned out that he'd actually had a heart attack.'

'And you've no idea what caused it?'

Jenny methodically wiped her fingers with the cleaning tissue provided. 'No, not the faintest – if I'm being strictly scientific; going by the book. Everything was pandemonium for the next couple of hours. Paramedics, police, the master, several fellows – the place was swarming and everyone was asking us what happened. All I wanted to do was get away. I felt sick . . . sick and guilty.'

Nat placed his hand over hers. 'You mustn't do that. It wasn't your fault that . . .'

She gave him a grateful smile and placed her other hand over his. 'Thanks for that, Nat. You're right, of course, but I'd give anything to know exactly what did happen. It seems so silly. I was only yards away from a man who met a violent death and yet I haven't a clue about what caused it.'

'It's an obvious question, but didn't the cameras show up anything?'

'Apparently not. I checked with Andy a couple of days later. He had the second-floor landing covered from two angles but he says there were no images on either camera.'

'Did the police check whether there was anyone else around?'

'Yes, they went into all the rooms and they cordoned off the staircase. There was a constable on duty when I eventually got away and I imagine he stayed all night. If anyone else had been lurking there I guess they'd have found him.'

'Well, there you are, then.' Nat smiled reassuringly. 'It was just a tragic accident. Hockridge simply missed his footing.'

'Yes, that's logical.' Jenny stared out of the window, frowning.

'But?' Nat prompted.

She turned to him and he read real anguish in her eyes. 'Nat, would you say that I was given to fantasizing?'

'Certainly not. You're one of the most level-headed students I've ever had.'

'I like to think that's true . . . So, why do I have this gut feeling that someone – or something – was involved in Hockridge's death? As I say, I'm trying to be scrupulously scientific even though part of me wants to believe in some sort of manifestation. So if I say I'm sure Hockridge experienced something that frightened him, am I just giving way to wishful thinking?'

Before Nat could offer any sort of an answer the boys returned, squabbling over the change they'd been given. Jenny looked at her watch, suddenly realized she was late meeting someone at the station and rushed out in search of a taxi.

When they got back to their home in Great Maddisham Kathryn was relaxing on the sofa hugging a mug of coffee. 'Hi guys,' she said. 'Good time?'

The boys stopped only to drop their bags on the floor

before rushing out to the garden. At the French window Jerry turned. 'Yes, we had a KFC and Daddy held hands with one of his girlfriends.'

Kathryn raised a quizzical eyebrow in her husband's direction and Nat wondered how to explain that he had decided not to return Zuylestein's letter.

The Second Day of Christmas – Later

Dear Dr Gye,

First, I must thank you for agreeing to help us. Secondly, I must remind you of the extreme sensitivity of the information I am about to share with you and beg you to treat it with the utmost confidentiality. This confidentiality extends to members of this college. For reasons which will become apparent, my approach to you has been made without the knowledge of other members of the governing body. I appreciate that this may well create difficulties for your enquiries but I am satisfied that your task would actually be impossible if your involvement became common knowledge.

The best way to provide you with such information as I have will be to relate past events as they appear from the vantage point of the present. Ten years ago, one of St Thomas's third-year Physics students was found dead in his room on F staircase. I understand from those who knew him that the young man, Paul Sutton, was extremely bright. It would, I gather, not have been inappropriate to use the word 'prodigy' to describe him. He was confidently expected to achieve a starred first in his finals and to stay here to read for a research degree. However, as I say, his life came to a tragic end a mere two weeks before he was due to begin his Part 2 Tripos exams. The police found evidence of drug abuse in his room and the pathologist had no doubt that death was due to a considerable heroin overdose. This all happened at a time when there was very grave anxiety about the spread of narcotic use among junior members of the university. In fact, the only good outcome of the Sutton affair was that it served as a powerful warning and provided something of a turning point in the war against the drug traffic in Cambridge.

This tragedy was, of course, an immense shock to the college and an even greater shock to the young man's family. Paul came from a quite humble background. He was an only child and his parents were immensely proud of him. In their grief they, not unnaturally, looked for someone to blame for the loss of their son. A lot of hard things were said about St Thomas's. The college had failed in its duty of care, had allowed suspected drug dealers on to the premises, had exerted too much academic pressure on a vulnerable student, etc. The governing body, of course, took all these criticisms very seriously but, as my colleagues assure me, there was little they could have done which might have averted the tragedy. Neither Paul's tutor nor his friends had any inkling that he had started using drugs and there were no indications that he was suffering an abnormal amount of stress. You will know better than most that tutors and supervisors are trained to look out for such things. This did not stop the coroner making one or two rather pointed remarks at the college's expense. He delivered a verdict of death by misadventure and the police were satisfied that no one else was involved in Paul's death. With that it seemed that a sad chapter in St Thomas's history had closed and things could return to normal.

It was decided to leave F5 untenanted for the next academic year, so it was eighteen months before the room had a new occupant. By then the proportion of female undergraduates was rising and F staircase was one of the areas provided for the young women. A certain Sarah Belman was the first one of them to be allocated to F5. She was, by all accounts, a rather highly strung, first-year student. One November night she ran screaming from her room and hammered on a friend's door, jabbering about hearing ghostly noises and seeing furniture move. Most of the fellows assumed that Sarah was the victim of a tasteless undergraduate prank but she absolutely refused to stay in F5, so the room was vacated again and remained empty for the rest of the year.

The next occupant apparently had no problems but a year further on the trouble began again and once more the college was obliged to re-accommodate the student lodged there. By now F5 was getting a reputation. You will, doubtless, recall an appalling piece of exploitative journalism in the local newspaper. An unprincipled reporter interviewed several junior members. He dragged up again the whole business of Paul Sutton's death and produced a sensationalist piece about the 'ghost of St Thomas's'. A myth was born and the college has been stuck with it ever since.

The most unfortunate aspect of this wretched business was that the Suttons became involved once more. The boy's mother convinced herself that the supposed 'manifestations' were her son's troubled spirit. She had never accepted the inquest's finding that Paul had been a drug addict and now she insisted that he would never be at peace until the truth had been established. A year or so ago she and her husband fell into the clutches of an unscrupulous lawyer who persuaded them that he could extract substantial 'compensation' from the college. Of course, he had no chance – at law – of doing any such thing, as our own legal experts made clear. What he could and did do was resort to what amounts to blackmail. He has used every means to keep the story in the public eye on the assumption that if he caused us enough embarrassment we would be forced to do a deal. Up to now we have called his bluff but his latest threat is potentially more damaging. He claims to have evidence that Paul Sutton was murdered and that the college has suppressed the details of his death. It is, of course, vile nonsense but he is in a strong position. He knows we cannot afford to let him pass his accusations to the media.

It was in order to regain the initiative that I authorized the Psychic Investigation Unit to set up their experiment. I thought that by commissioning a scientific study we would demonstrate that St Thomas's was taking the whole issue seriously. If the result was negative, as it would, surely, be, we might be able to scotch this 'ghost' nonsense once and for all. Well, that plan has certainly backfired on us with a vengeance. Hockridge's accident has provided sackfuls of grist to Tyrone's mill. (Tyrone is the name of the rogue solicitor – I see that I omitted to mention that above.)

You will now realize, Dr Gye, the parlous position the college finds itself in. We are currently in the midst of highly important negotiations with a wealthy potential benefactor. We have to upgrade our accommodation drastically in order to attract the conference trade without which colleges cannot survive today. We have earmarked part of any new funds to a complete refurbishment of the rooms on D, E and F staircases. That should lay any ghost nonsense once and for all. We cannot allow this sordid business to dash our plans. The governing body, almost to a man, is in favour of doing a deal with Tyrone. I have failed to convince them that to do so would be to put ourselves wholly in his power. That is why my approach to you is couched in such seemingly melodramatic secrecy. The festive season has given us a very brief breathing space but I can only stall for a couple of weeks. On 6 January we have our Epiphany Feast – a St Thomas's tradition. It is always preceded by a meeting at which we review the past year's progress. I have invited our potential benefactor to meet my colleagues and to see for himself that the college is in good heart.

What I am asking of you is difficult, perhaps impossible. I can only hope that you will do your best on our behalf. For that both I and the college will be extremely grateful.

Yours sincerely,
Joseph Zuylestein

Sitting at his desk that evening Nat went through the letter four times. At each reading his spirits sank lower. He mentally cursed the Master of St Thomas's for dragging him into the internal politics of the college. It took little reading between the lines to see that the fellows of St Tom's were at war with their new master and that anyone who ventured on to the no-man's-land between them was likely to be shot at from both sides. As for Sir Joseph's demand for secrecy, how could Nat be expected to make enquiries without rumours of what he was doing leaking out? 'Perhaps impossible', Zuylestein had written. 'No perhaps about it,' Nat muttered. Still, as the explorer Nansen once said, 'The difficult is what takes a little time; the impossible is what takes a little longer.' With a sigh, Nat turned his attention to his computer keyboard. Having opened up the machine, he typed in the keyword 'Journal'.

It was his conscientious custom to keep notes on everything that might some time be of use in his teaching or television work. Now, he painstakingly transferred the master's letter *in toto* to a new file headed 'St Thomas's College' and linked it to 'Psychic Investigation'. Over the years he had developed a technique of using the screen as a disembodied mind with which he could hold a dialogue. Now he posed it questions and bounced some ideas off it.

Paul Sutton: How to find out about him without alerting anyone at St Tom's? Can't talk to his tutor. Parents? Undergraduate contemporaries? Should be possible if we come up with a feasible excuse. Survey of student deaths in the university? Involve Jenny?

Events Surrounding Hockridge's Death: Talk with Andy Rowsell? What chance of him co-operating? Ask Jenny. Thorough examination of F5. Any way someone could be concealed there? If Jenny's intuition right Hockridge must have seen or heard something which startled him.

Tyrone: Could be useful to obtain background information on the dodgy lawyer. If there was some way of warning him off that would solve Zuylestein's problem and get me off the hook. Could be a job for Barny Cox.

Nat yawned and pushed his chair back from the desk. He realized that he was no longer feeling utterly despondent. Perhaps Nansen was right.

In the bedroom Kathryn was already installed in the wide bed, the coverlet around her strewn with exuberantly coloured pictures on A3 card.

'You look busy,' Nat said, beginning to undress.

'April cover designs,' Kathryn muttered.

As editor of *Panache*, the international fashion/gossip magazine, she was an extremely busy woman but also able to do a high proportion of her work from home.

34

'Beats me how you manage always to be thinking months ahead,' Nat said. 'Here we are in typical sub-arctic Cambridge winter, with a wind blowing straight from the Urals, and you're focusing your mind on "the flowers that bloom in the spring, trala". So, what will you be telling all the beautiful people to wear this Easter?'

'You make them sound like Pavlov's dogs.' Kathryn gathered the cards together and dropped them on the floor beside her.

Nat pulled on his pyjama jacket and slipped into bed. 'Well, they are, in a way – people whose lives are so humdrum that they're easy prey to the fashion gurus who, in their turn, have their strings pulled by the rag trade.'

Kathryn glowered at him. 'Then, I suppose that makes me some kind of Svengali.'

'No, I didn't mean . . .'

'What's brought on this cynical mood? What have you been working on?'

'This wretched St Tom's business.'

'Taking it seriously, now?'

'I suppose I have to. You were right about it.'

'Are you doing it for my sake or your "girlfriend's"?'

Nat laughed. 'Jerry's a mischievous brat!'

'Still, out of the mouths of babes . . . and so on. What did little Jennifer say to change your mind?'

'She's still in shock over the Hockridge business. It's not every day that a senior member of the university drops dead at your feet. She's got it into her head that someone else was involved in the professor's death.'

'Why does she think that?'

Nat shrugged. 'Feminine intuition?'

'I thought you didn't believe in that.'

Nat ignored the barb. 'Jenny was the only real witness to what happened. She was closest to Hockridge in the seconds before he fell. Something about it seemed . . . wrong, odd. She can't put her finger on it. Now, it may be that there's nothing for her to remember. On the other hand, her unconscious might have erected a barrier. If that's the case the chances are that it will eventually come down. Then we might get some idea of why a middle-aged don took a fatal tumble down a staircase.'

'It hasn't occurred to you that Jenny might be exaggerating all this in order to spend some time with you?'

'No. Why should it?'

'Because she's been sweet on you ever since you tutored her for her PhD.'

Nat struggled to control his irritation. 'Oh, for goodness sake! If there's any truth in that – and I don't think there is – *I* wasn't sweet on *her* and I'm certainly not now. Anyway, Jenny's vague misgiving isn't the only reason for getting involved in the St Tom's business. You've read Zuylestein's letter. Someone's trying to screw money out of the college and, what's worse, they've battened on to the grief of parents who have lost a son. That is so despicable. If I can do anything to spike this Tyrone fellow's guns then I should.'

'Zuylestein could go to the police.'

'And tell them what? There's no fresh evidence to make them reopen the investigation into Hockridge's death and no reason for them to get out the old files on Paul Sutton's.'

'But if Tyrone claims to have found new evidence the police can make him reveal it.'

'Oh, I'm sure he'll have been clever enough not to put anything in writing. And, in any case, St Tom's can't afford the publicity of having the Sutton case raked over again. No, Tyrone's got them over a barrel. Anyway,' he slid down beneath the sheets, 'time to get some sleep, unless . . .' He put out a hand to his wife's shoulder.

'Yes, you're right. I'm whacked. Goodnight.' She turned over with her back towards him.

The Third Day of Christmas

The next morning Nat went to his study straight after breakfast and was busy on the telephone for more than an hour. The first result was a hastily arranged lunch meeting at the Lamb, Frettlingham. The pub, in a hollow beside the diminutive, meandering Frett, was a couple of miles from Great Maddisham and a favourite, quiet eating and drinking place of the Gyes. On a cold afternoon at the year's end it was almost deserted. Nat had counted on that. As he entered the long bar at a little after twelve thirty he glanced approvingly round at the empty tables. His choice of venue had been a nod in the direction of Zuylestein's insistence on discretion. He was about to flout the master's admonition not to open to anyone else the problems of St Thomas's. It was a decision he had reached with a clear conscience. If he was to tackle Zuylestein's problem within the absurdly short timeframe he had been given he could not do it single-handed.

Wendy Hawke, the well-built co-licensee, looked up from the newspaper she was reading behind the bar as he entered. 'Good Lord, a customer,' she said with a grin. 'Hello, Nat. Good Christmas?'

'Great fun but I'm glad it's over. Any chance of a lunch which doesn't have any trace of turkey in it?'

Wendy pulled a face. 'Menu's a bit on the short side at the moment. I'm on my own in the kitchen. Well, there's not much point bringing staff in this side of New Year. I can do you a ploughman's, or soop doo joor – that's mushroom and it hasn't come out of a tin.'

'As if I'd suspect anything you serve as being canned, Wendy.'

'The day I can't be bothered to cook proper is the day I'll retire. Now, what I have got on the hob,' she lowered her voice to a conspiratorial whisper, even though the only other occupants of the bar were two elderly drinkers engaged in their own conversation and well out of earshot, 'is a nice pheasant stew, done in burgundy with herbs and whatnot. It's my version of cock o van.'

'Sounds fabulous. I'm sure the Judge will go for that, too. He's joining me for lunch. And there'll also be a young lady. I can't vouch for her taste.'

At that moment Jenny Collard strode in, throwing the hood of her anorak back from her dark hair and pulling off woollen gloves. 'Hello, Nat,' she said, coming across to the bar. 'It's biting cold out there and I've had the wind against me all the way.'

'Have you cycled from Cambridge?' Nat asked, looking at her reddened cheeks. 'I could have picked you up if you'd said.'

'Wouldn't have dreamed of it. Cycling keeps me fit – that and a regular workout. Anyway, since you offered me lunch I wanted to build up a good appetite.'

A few minutes later the third member of the party arrived. Barny Cox was a tall, spruce, retired member of Cambridge's legal faculty. The luxuriant white hair brushed back from his narrow face gave him an appearance that managed to be at the same time both distinguished and raffish. Only in the confines of the Lamb did anyone dare refer to Barny as 'the Judge'.

'Greetings, Nathaniel. How pleasant to be summoned out of the post-Christmas doldrums.'

The newcomer cast an inquisitive glance in Jenny's direction and Nat made the introductions.

The trio placed their order and retired to a corner table. As soon as they were settled Nat told his companions the reason for their gathering. For Barny's information he went over the events leading up to Hockridge's death. Then he went over the salient points of the master's letter.

The revelations of St Thomas's problems brought a gleam to Jenny's eyes. 'So that's why they were suddenly so keen to involve the PIU,' she said. 'We asked once before for permission to investigate. All we got was a brush-off. And not a very polite one, either. Then old Zuylestein phoned in person and couldn't have been more helpful. He tried to make it sound as though he was doing *us* a favour but I knew there was much more to it than a sudden conversion. Now, I get the picture.'

'There you are, my dears. Help yourselves!' Wendy plonked down a steaming casserole in the middle of the table and returned moments later with three plates. 'You'll have to slum it today – no staff,' she muttered before bustling away.

'That smells fantastic!' Jenny enthused, eagerly spooning out stew. 'How'd you guys find this place? I've never heard of it.'

Barny frowned. 'It's a little secret we like to keep. If the urban multitudes were to get wind of it there would be raucous musak, pin-ball machines and shaven-haired youths on motorbikes here in next to no time. I trust we can count on your discretion, young lady.'

'Cross my heart and hope to die,' Jenny responded with a grin.

The food was delicious and, for some minutes, received their full attention. It was Barny who brought them back to the subject of St Tom's.

'Well, my dear Nathaniel, I'd say you've bitten off more than you can chew this time.'

'It'd be more accurate to say I've had it thrust down my throat. But you're right,' Nat conceded. 'The problem is bigger than I can tackle and that's why I need help.'

'Well, as you know, I'm ever the eager foot soldier,' Barny said.

'Count me in, too.' Jenny nodded enthusiastically. 'What are our marching orders?'

'Well, as I see it, there are two lines of approach. We need to find out all we can about Paul Sutton, and it would be useful to discover what evidence this unsavoury Tyrone character thinks he's come up with.'

'I take it you'd like me to tackle the lawyer?' Barny asked.

Nat nodded. 'I can't imagine you'll get much out of him. He sounds like a pretty hardboiled character. But it's worth a try. I suppose the best solution all round would be if we could come up with something unpleasant against Tyrone. A bit of counter-blackmail might warn him off and we'd have fulfilled our obligation to St Tom's.'

Barny raised bushy eyebrows. 'You want me to dish the dirt on a fellow member of the profession.'

'Something like that.' Nat grinned.

'It'll be a pleasure. The likes of Tyrone are the dry rot of the legal system. As it happens, I've recently been appointed to a Law Society commission on the compensation culture. I have carte blanche to interview members of the "No claim, no fee" brigade. I think I might rather enjoy putting the frighteners on friend Tyrone.'

Jenny had been listening impatiently to this exchange. 'So where do I fit in to the grand design?' she asked.

'Well, it would be good to see your notes on the F5 phenomena and I thought you might also chase up some of Paul Sutton's contemporaries. They'd be sure to remember the dramatic details of his death.'

Jenny pulled a face. 'No problem about the file. I'll email it to you when I get back. But, hey, I'm not that old. The Sutton business was before my time.'

'You could get names from college registers then make a few judicious phone calls. Say you're doing a post-doctoral thesis on student stress.'

She still looked doubtful. 'Yeah, I suppose . . . but what am I looking for?'

Nat shrugged. 'Anything and everything. This is straw-clutching time. The official story is that everyone was taken aback when Sutton OD'd. By all accounts he wasn't that sort of a chap. You might have a go at testing that theory. All we're trying to do is back up the official coroner's verdict. If our brilliant Master Paul *was* messing about with heroin some of his friends must have known. They were probably dabbling too. They wouldn't have wanted to admit it at the time but after all these years the revelation can't do them any harm. If we could just find a couple of people prepared to swear that Sutton was a user that might take the sting out of whatever evidence Tyrone thinks he's come up with.'

Barny brought his keen eyes to bear on Nat across the table. 'And while the minions are thus occupied what will the *chef de bureau* be doing?'

'Don't worry, Barny. I have allocated myself the short straw.'

'The still-grieving parents?'

'Yes. I'll see if I can talk them out of this "troubled spirit" business.'

'A tall order, surely. Won't they be clinging desperately to the belief that their son is trying to communicate from the "other side" in an attempt to clear his name? As well as their sense of loss they'll have a great deal of family pride tied up proving that their only child wasn't a drug addict.'

'Undoubtedly.'

'But they might be right.'

Both men turned to stare at Jenny.

She said, 'You seem to be making the assumption that there isn't and never has been any paranormal activity on F staircase. As far as I'm concerned, the jury's still out.'

Barny smiled benignly. 'Ah, the ever-open scientific mind.'

'Certainly!' Jenny looked daggers at him. 'And I've now remembered what was bothering me about old Prof Hockridge's tumble down the stairs. But if you two have already made up your minds . . .'

Nat said quietly, 'We're ruling nothing out, Jenny. Right now we're blundering about in the dark without a candle.

41

Any flicker of light would be more than welcome. What have you remembered?'

'It was my first reaction.' Jenny closed her eyes in concentration.

'What do you mean by "first reaction", Jenny?' Nat asked.

'Well, I saw Hockridge fall backwards and land on the floor at my feet and then, of course, I was only interested in checking whether he was all right. It was only yesterday that it came back to me what I saw and felt *before* that. The old fool went rushing up the stairs. He turned the bend and then, just as he did so, he screamed and lunged forward.'

'Forward!' Nat exclaimed. 'You're sure?'

'Yes. It was only momentary but I've gone over it time and again. He put his arms out straight in front of him.'

'As though warding something off?' Nat asked.

'Or attacking someone?' Barny suggested.

Jenny shook her head. 'It was all too quick. My immediate thought was that he saw *something*. But,' she shrugged, 'according to all Andy's expensive gear, there was absolutely nothing on the staircase.'

'Probably his own shadow,' Barny suggested dismissively.

'I suppose,' Jenny admitted. 'And yet, I dunno. The way he set off up the stairs . . . He was convinced we were a bunch of idiots and he was hell-bent on proving it. If it had been Little Cynth . . . well, she was a bundle of nerves; ready to jump at the squeak of a mouse. But the professor? Not exactly the sort of person to throw a fit of the heebie-jeebies.'

Nat said, 'It's worth checking. Would Andy mind you looking at his video footage?'

Jenny laughed. 'He'd mind like hell but that's not going to put me off. It was my investigation and I'd be happy of a chance to make that one hundred per cent clear.'

On the way back to Great Maddisham, Nat turned over the problem of how to approach the Suttons. Barny had been absolutely right that engaging their support would be a 'tall order'. There was one key that, in Nat's experience, often opened stubborn doors. He did not like using his television celebrity to gain access to people's confidence. In fact it was, in his view, nothing short of immoral. But, with time pressing . . .

From his study he put a call through to Susan Avery-White's mobile phone. Susan was the production assistant on the latest series of *Is There Anybody There?*, Nat's occasional investigative series on the paranormal.

'I'll try,' the ever-amenable Sue replied when Nat told her what he wanted. 'But I've only got today and tomorrow. We're off at the end of the week. Trying to grab a few days skiing before the next round of pre-production meetings start. Give me the number and I'll see what the magic of television can do.'

'This is very good of you, Sue. I've no right to ask it.'

He heard a sigh at the other end of the line. 'Oh, I reckon I'll think of some way for you to make it up to me.'

Within the hour she phoned back. 'All fixed,' she said. 'They're expecting your call.'

The following afternoon Nat made the one-hour journey to Watford. He spent much of the drive down the sparsely occupied A1(M) thinking black thoughts about Sir Joseph Zuylestein. It was a way of working off his own guilt. He hated what he was about to do. It was shabby. It was dishonest. He derived no comfort from the fact that it was standard behaviour in the media world. In the endless pursuit of personal anecdotes and expertise that could be used to bolster the reputations of producers and presenters, researchers were quite ruthless in invading private lives and holding out the prospect of five minutes of fame to would-be contributors. Then, when they had gleaned the information they required for the script (at no cost to the production budget) they quietly forgot the 'ordinary', 'dull' people who had provided it. It was a professional practice Nat had sometimes protested about – and here he was doing the same thing himself. Only, of course, it was not his fault. It was all down to that bloody man Zuylestein.

Nat knew long before he reached it what 43 Plimstock Rise would look like. He envisaged the 1930s, three-bedroomed semi with its few square yards of grassed front garden and, to one side, the garage built to accommodate cars that were smaller than their modern counterparts.

'We ought to move to somewhere smaller. There's more room here than we need . . . but . . . you know . . .' Gerald Sutton responded to Nat's compliment about the neatness of the house as he led the way across the hall. He was a tall, thin man with black-grey hair and a permanently worried expression. In the lounge he hovered uncertainly as Nat took his seat in one of the two leather armchairs. 'Jane . . . the wife . . . she'll be back soon. She's helping with a children's party at the church hall.' Sutton waved a hand at the cups and saucers and plates laid out on a low table. 'Left me to do the honours, I'm afraid.'

'Perhaps we should wait for her,' Nat suggested.

'No, no, Jane wouldn't hear of it. She said you'd be ready for a cuppa after your journey. I'll just nip out to the kitchen . . . the kettle . . .' Sutton sidled through the doorway leaving the sentence hanging almost visibly in the air.

Nat looked around the room which ran the length of the ground floor from front bay window to French doors giving on to a patio. Everything was immaculate and bore the stamp of the obsessively house-proud wife. Walls and doors were crisply papered and painted. Nat imagined Gerald being pressed into a Forth Bridge programme of constant re-decoration. Curtains and carpets were quietly tasteful and did not clash. There were enough ornaments to add interest but not too many to create clutter. Only one item was missing. Nat scanned the walls, mantelpiece and window ledges in vain for any photographs.

'Here we are.' Gerald returned bearing the teapot like a newly presented sports trophy. 'Now, Dr Gye, how do you take your tea?'

'Milk, no sugar,' Nat responded, 'and, please, everyone calls me Nathaniel or Nat.'

'Oh ... er ... right, Nathaniel, you've no idea what a surprise it was when your young lady phoned to say you wanted to feature our story on your programme. Jane is a big fan of yours. I must be honest and tell you that I haven't actually seen ... Don't watch much telly, really ... The news and gardening programmes mostly ... Never seem to have much time ... the garden, you know ... and my wood-carving ...'

'Wood-carving?' Nat thankfully spotted a conversation topic that would, hopefully, put his host more at ease. 'What sort of things do you make?'

Sutton shrugged. 'Oh, just bits and pieces. I don't suppose you'd ... Anyway, they're out in the shed. Jane says they make too much clutter indoors.'

'I'd be very interested to see your work. There might be a useful visual angle there for the programme. Showing people in their natural environment helps us to convey character; present people the audience can identify with.' Nat searched for a way to turn attention to Paul Sutton 'Did your son share this hobby?'

The response was sharp. 'Paul? Oh no!' Nat noticed the very brief, almost sardonic curl of Sutton's upper lip. 'Manual skills weren't in his line. Everything happened up here.' He tapped his forehead.

'Always very bright, was he?'

'Bright?' Sutton paused, staring out of the window, as though weighing up all the implications of the word before committing himself to a definitive answer. 'What is genius, Dr Gye? Er, sorry, Nathaniel. You must come across it quite often in your university. I mean, is it just a question of being extra clever ... five per cent, ten per cent brainier than everyone else in the class? Or is it something different ... special?' Sutton shook his head, as though surprised at his own loquaciousness.

'That's not an easy one to answer,' Nat said. 'Paul was in the genius category, was he?'

'That was what some of his teachers reckoned. It wasn't that clear to Jane and me at first . . . you know, seeing him every day – his ups and downs, his tantrums, his fads. For all we knew all kids were like that. We didn't have any others to compare him with, you see. I sometimes think that if Paul had had brothers and sisters . . .' Again the sentence faded away like Sullivan's 'Lost Chord'.

'When did it dawn on you that he was different?'

Sutton wrinkled his forehead, pondering the question. 'I suppose he'd have been about ten. His primary head-teacher called us in for a chat. Said we ought to think very carefully about the next stage of his education. He warned us off the local comprehensive. "Paul won't fit in there," he said.'

'He went on to a private school?'

'Yes. Paul was mad keen to go to a boarding school but that wasn't possible . . . not on the wages of a grade two clerk. Still, we're lucky here. William Barton College is only five miles away and they take day boys. He did very well there . . . I'm sure that was the right decision.'

Nat wondered who Sutton was trying to convince. He said, 'Have you any photos of Paul? We'll need some stills for the programme.'

'Photos?' Sutton seemed taken aback by the word. 'Er . . . yes . . . They're upstairs . . .'

'If that's a problem we can deal with it at a later stage, when we've worked out the shape of the programme. I just thought . . .'

'No, no, Dr Gye, that's OK.' He stood up. 'You'd better come up and see . . .' He turned abruptly to the door.

Nat followed him up the staircase. On the landing Sutton took out a key and opened a bedroom door. 'This is . . . was . . . Paul's room.' He switched on the light.

Nat took a step across the threshold, then froze. He was in what was obviously the largest of 43 Plimstock Rise's three bedrooms. Heavy curtains were drawn across the windows, hence the need for electric light. As he stood in the doorway, taking in the scene, he heard Sutton's apologetic voice behind him. 'It was a terrible shock, you see. We couldn't bring ourselves . . .'

To change anything. Nat mentally finished the sentence for him. He was intruding on a shrine. The room had all the rational untidiness of a real personality; someone who had, perhaps, just got up from the desk against the right-hand wall and would at any moment return. Books, magazines and papers were everywhere – on the desk, the floor, the bedside table, the crammed shelves between the windows and bed's crumpled coverlet. Could this really be how Paul Sutton had left his sanctum more than ten years ago? No, Nat thought, first impressions were deceptive. This was an *arranged* display, a 'stage set' designed to capture and keep perpetually imprisoned the essence of Jane's and Gerald's lost son. For one thing there were the photographs. Nat could see why there were no images of Paul downstairs; they were all here. The walls were covered with his pictures – everything from snapshots to school groups and studio portraits.

Nat advanced to examine some of them, wondering what these curling rectangles of glossy card could tell him about the young man whose death had set in train all the troubles at St Tom's. He studied what appeared to be the more recent photos. They showed a slim, fair-haired youth of medium height, with a face which tapered from a broad forehead to a pointed chin. Sometimes he was bespectacled, sometimes not. Every picture seemed to be posed. Paul appeared looking up from his desk, leaning out of a window, standing on the steps leading to the hall at St Thomas's, lounging against the balustrade of Clare Bridge. What struck Nat immediately was that in all the photographs Paul appeared alone. He looked at some of the earlier pictures. Almost without exception they were the same. Only the earliest photographs were typical family album snapshots showing Paul as a child with family members or friends.

47

'It seems lots of people wanted to take Paul's photo,' he observed.

'Not really.' Gerald hovered in the doorway.

'But . . .' Nat waved a hand at the gallery.

'He took most of them himself . . . Timed shutter release . . . He was a keen photographer . . .Which ones will you want for the programme?'

Nat explained that the production team would decide on the visuals they wanted to use. 'But thanks for showing me this. It's a great help. I'll be able to give them a good idea of what's here.'

'Right . . . If you've seen all you . . . We'd better go back down . . . Jane . . .'

In fact it was as they descended the stairs that the front door opened and a diminutive woman in a black topcoat came in. Jane Sutton stopped in the open doorway, staring up at her husband. The unspoken message communicated itself, for Gerald halted momentarily then said hurriedly, 'Dear, this is Dr Gye. He needs pictures and things for his programme. That's why I've . . .'

'Been showing him Paul's room,' Jane Sutton said. Nat realized why Gerald had got out of the habit of completing his own sentences.

Jane closed the door behind her and held out her hand. 'Pleased to meet you, Dr Gye.' The smile was only on the surface. The eyes wary. 'I hope Gerald hasn't been raising your hopes. We haven't decided definitely to take part in your programme. Nothing personal, of course. I enjoy your series very much. It's just that Gerald and I wanted to have a preliminary discussion with you to see whether we want to go ahead.'

'Of course,' Nat said. 'We never go into production with any story – however promising – if the people involved are not one hundred per cent happy about it.' As he turned to re-enter the lounge he caught a glimpse of the scowl Jane directed at her husband.

When they were seated again, Jane Sutton presided over

her own tea table, her authority over this domestic empire fully restored. Gerald, deep in his armchair, was just as completely submerged in silence.

Nat tried to get the conversation moving in the required direction. 'Your son's tragic story and its strange aftermath are extremely interesting. I do hope you will allow us to feature them. Cambridge is full of ghost stories, as I expect you can imagine. Good material for the tourist guides but little more. This phenomenon at St Thomas's has some unusual features.'

'Paul will never rest until the truth about his death comes out.' Jane's unflinching gaze was a challenge which sent the message, 'Don't even think about contradicting me.'

Nat sidestepped. 'Could we go over the events of ten years ago – if it's not too painful for you.'

'I'll tell you what *didn't* happen, Dr Gye: our Paul did *not* take heroin.'

'I see,' Nat said quietly. 'Then what . . .'

'Really happened? He was murdered and the person who murdered him used drugs to make it look like an accidental overdose.'

'Then, Paul must have had a very ruthless and determined enemy. Did he give you any indication that that might be?'

Jane gave a disconsolate shake of the head and looked across at her husband.

Gerald said, 'Paul wasn't at home much, not even in the vacations.'

Jane hurriedly amplified: 'He had his work and he made lots of friends in Cambridge. He often spent his holidays with them. We encouraged him, of course.'

'So you've no idea what really happened?' Nat asked.

'Well, if we haven't it's not for want of trying,' Jane said truculently. 'But we could never get anything out of the college. Shut up like a door, they did. They've got something to hide and we won't stop till we find out the truth.'

It was Gerald who broke the awkward silence that followed. 'We thought your programme might ... you know ... shake things up a bit.'

'The threat of being exposed on television should make them come clean.'

'I shouldn't bank on that, Mrs Sutton,' Nat said. 'What we shall be doing – *if* we use your story – is considering the evidence for paranormal activity. We don't do criminal investigations.'

'But at least it might make those toffee-nosed, arrogant snobs talk to us. They've always refused up to now.'

Nat tried to get the conversation on to the involvement of Tyrone. 'I suspect the only thing that would make them change their attitude is positive evidence that the college was negligent or even culpable in the matter of your son's death. I assume you don't have such evidence.'

He realized immediately, from Jane's sharp, suspicious glance, that he had gone too far.

'We might and we might not,' she said. 'For the moment we're saying nothing. We'll show our hand in our own good time.'

'Quite right, too,' Nat said. 'I'd better explain how we go about putting a programme together – let you know what you might be in for.'

Nat spent the next twenty minutes or so explaining production procedures. Then he said his 'thank yous', promised to be back in touch shortly and took his leave.

On the drive back to Cambridge he had much to ponder on what had been said – and what had not been said.

The Fourth Day of Christmas

Mr Peter Tyrone bitterly resented being summoned to open his office in the middle of the Christmas–New Year holiday. That much was absolutely clear before he opened his mouth – although he lost little time in doing just that. He emerged from a black Range Rover dressed in a brown suede jacket and jeans and crossed the pavement to where Barny Cox was waiting outside the glass door bearing the sign, 'Critchley, Critchley and Tyrone'.

'You must be Cox,' he announced. 'What's all this about? I'm supposed to be at the coast working on my boat.'

Barny surveyed the thirty-something figure with the close-cropped hair and self-assertive air and disapproved of what he saw. In his book flashy solicitors were as much an anathema as trendy vicars. Clients expected – and were entitled to – a measure of decorum in their legal representatives.

He said, 'Good afternoon, Mr Tyrone. This shouldn't take long – if all goes well.'

'What's that supposed to mean? Are you suggesting . . .?'

'Shall we step inside?'

Tyrone led the way through an outer office into his own domain and planted himself in the swivel chair behind the desk. 'You'd better keep your coat on. We don't waste money on heating during staff holidays,' he announced.

'It's important to be cost conscious,' Barny said. 'Business good?' He wandered round the room, peering at the neat shelves of box files.

'Pretty average, I suppose, for a provincial firm. We get by. Look here, what's this . . .'

'Mainly conveyancing and probate, I suppose?'

'Yes. Look here, Cox, I really don't have time . . .'

'Not much court work, then?'

'A bit. I like to keep my hand in with litigation.'

Barny turned – a sudden movement. 'Right, let's get down to work, shall we?' He noticed with pleasure the worried frown on the lawyer's sharp features. 'It's your record in civil prosecutions that we're interested in. You were being unduly modest about your firm's activity in this area, weren't you? Certain . . . *comments* – "complaints" would be too strong a word – have reached the Society's headquarters.'

'That's ridiculous! There's absolutely nothing . . .'

Barny held up an imperious hand and the other man fell silent.

'I'm not here to make any accusations, Mr Tyrone. Just to check a few facts. You will be aware that the profession has been attracting something of a bad press over what is popularly called "the compensation culture".'

The other man looked relieved. 'Oh, you mean the "No win, no fee" merchants. Yes, very unsavoury. You won't find anything of that sort on our books.'

'You don't handle compensation suits?'

Tyrone shrugged. 'Now and again. Now and again. If people find themselves up against obstructive bureaucrats or faceless corporations they need all the help they can get.'

'So, you see yourself as a disinterested champion of the little man?'

Tyrone looked up with a smile. 'Isn't that part of our job?'

Barny stared back and made no response. It was obvious that the smarmy young lawyer was unlikely to let anything slip. He would have to be confronted directly about his interest in the Sutton case. While he framed a question he turned to pick up his briefcase from beside the door. It was then he noticed something that made him do a quick rethink.

52

When he left the solicitor's office some twenty minutes later with the assurance that he would be making a preliminary report and might have to return with more questions, he had said nothing about the real purpose of his visit.

On his return home from Watford Nat went straight to his study. He wanted to enter the new information in his computer journal while it was fresh in his mind.

> Paul Sutton: an only child. Must have been born when his parents were already in their mid-to-later thirties. They doted on him – mother especially. Unhealthy situation. Ten years after his death mother keeps his room as a shrine.
>
> What does his early upbringing suggest? Ego constantly fed by Mama. Boy smothered by love. He wanted to escape to boarding school but that wasn't possible. Lack of money or tightly tied apron strings? Probably a spoiled brat who repaid parental love with temper tantrums and eventually contempt. Totally self-absorbed. His room was plastered with photos of himself.

The phone rang. Before Nat could pick up the receiver it stopped. Seconds later Kathryn called up the stairs. 'It's for you!'

'Who is it?' he shouted back.

'The delectable Jenny.'

Nat lifted the handset. 'Hello, Jenny.'

'Nat, hi!' She sounded breathless. 'I've just got back from Norwich. I collected my bike at the station and was just cycling home when I thought I could come over to see you now.'

'Well, I . . . Is it that important?'

'You bet. I found out quite a lot about Paul Sutton. Look, I can be at your place in half an hour or so.'

'No, you mustn't cycle all this way in the dark. I'll come and fetch you.' They arranged a pick-up point.

53

Nat went downstairs. Kathryn and the boys were playing a card game.

'Queen, king, ace!' Jerry threw the cards down triumphantly. 'I win again.'

His mother laughed. 'Yes, you're quite invincible today. Here's your dad come to join us. Let's see if he can beat you.'

'Bet he can't,' the younger boy said. 'I'm invincible.' He relished the word.

'Bet he can,' his brother said, jumping up and skipping across to his father.

Kathryn stood up. 'I must get supper ready. Have a couple of rounds with them, Nat. See if you can't stop Jerry turning into an inveterate gambler.'

Nat shook his head ruefully. 'Not just at the moment, I'm afraid. I've just got to nip out.' He saw the boys' faces fall. 'Later on, I promise. Just before bed time.'

'Where are you off to?' Kathryn asked from the kitchen doorway.

'I'm just going to fetch Jenny. She says she's found out something about the St Tom's business. I thought we could give her a bite of supper. That's OK, isn't it?'

Kathryn turned abruptly and went into the kitchen. 'Why not?' she called back over her shoulder.

Forty minutes later, when the five of them were sitting round the dining table, the conversation did not exactly flow smoothly. When the boys had retired to Jerry's room to play computer games, Nat said, 'We're beginning to get some kind of profile on Paul Sutton. Jenny and I have found some bits of the jigsaw that seem to fit together.'

Kathryn got up from the table. 'Then I'll leave you to your puzzle.'

Nat said, 'Don't you want to hear about our progress?'

'I'd better tidy up the kitchen.' She flashed a surface smile at Jenny. 'No au pair till after the holiday. Tell me all about it later, Darling.' She closed the kitchen door behind her.

Jenny looked bemused. 'Was it a bad idea – coming over this evening?' she asked *sotto voce*.

'No, it's OK. I was going to suggest tomorrow but we've got so little time. We can't afford a leisurely approach. Now, you were telling me in the car about this woman you met in Norwich. What was her name?'

'Sandra Cowley – Dr Sandra Cowley. Nice woman. Sensible. Unflappable. The sort of person you'd have every confidence in as a GP.'

'And she was contemporary with Paul Sutton at St Tom's?'

'No, she was at Newnham reading medicine. She came across our young man socially. A friend of hers – Anne something-or-other – I've got a note somewhere – went out with Paul for a while.'

'So, how did the trail lead to Norwich?'

Jenny leaned forward across the table. 'Not so much following a trail as answering a summons,' she said. 'I phoned a friend of mine called Josh who works for the *East Anglian Courier*. I thought he'd be a good person to start with. He has fingers in several pies. He said he'd make a few enquiries and get back to me. The next I knew I got this call from Sandra Cowley. She gave me quite a grilling. Wanted to know why I was interested in Paul Sutton after all these years.'

'You gave her the post-doctoral thesis story?'

'Yes. I'm not sure she believed me. Anyway, she eventually invited me to go and see her. We met in her surgery. Very quiet. Very private. ' Jenny stopped, a thoughtful frown on her face.

'And?' Nat prompted.

'Sorry. It's just that I've been trying to sort out what it was all about.'

'What *what* was all about? You're talking in riddles, Jenny.'

She shook her head. 'Yes, I suppose I am. Sorry. Well, I was there about an hour and Dr Cowley was talking pretty well all that time. I mean, there was I, a complete stranger, and it was as though she wanted to unburden herself.'

Nat struggled with impatience. 'What did she actually *say*?'

'She said that Paul Sutton was the nastiest piece of work it had ever been her misfortune to come across. She reckons he really deserved what he got.'

'You don't suppose she . . .'

Jenny shook her head. 'No, though, God knows, she had cause enough.'

'Tell me about it.'

'Well, her friend, Anne, introduced them and Dr Cowley took an instant dislike to him. By her reckoning he was immensely conceited. She said he thought he wasn't just God's gift to women; he was God's gift to the world. He had a big following – not so much friends as disciples, Dr Cowley said. It was probably the money that attracted them.'

'Money? Paul was well off, then.'

'Mmm. Always splashing it around, apparently.'

'Interesting.' Nat pictured the modest semi in Watford. 'I wonder where that came from.'

'I'll get to that in a moment. The image he projected was of a fun guy who enjoyed throwing parties – usually discreet affairs for a handful of favoured acolytes. The rumour was that "orgies" might have been a better word. He tried to draw Sandra Cowley into his inner circle. She wasn't having any. He persisted. He wasn't accustomed to rejection. Took it as a challenge. She was level-headed enough not to be flattered by his attentions. It took her some months to work out why he was so interested. He seemed to be particularly fascinated by her contacts at the hospital and it eventually dawned on her that she'd introduced him to a number of her med student friends and some of the nurses.'

Nat nodded. 'Do I smell an interest in drugs?'

'Yes. So did Sandra eventually. She says she could have kicked herself for not spotting it earlier. She realized that several of Paul's circle were using – some just pot, but others more serious substances. She worked out that Paul was the supplier and she confronted him.'

56

'He must have known he couldn't get away with it indefinitely.'

'Dr Cowley says he didn't bat an eyelid. He really believed he was fireproof. He told her that he could and would do whatever he wanted. There was no one clever enough or strong enough to stand in his way. He sounds like a classic example of Narcissistic Personality Disorder.'

'Did Sandra report him to the college authorities?'

Jenny's freckled nose wrinkled in a scowl. 'No. She threatened to but he turned the tables on her. If she blabbed, he'd claim that she was one of his sources of illegal substances.'

Nat snorted. 'He'd never get away with that. He was obviously bluffing!'

'Oh no, he was too smart for that. He had a genuine hold over her.'

'What was that?'

'Her elder brother was a top-class athlete. Actually went on to take a bronze medal in the Sydney Olympics. Sutton said he only had to drop the word "drugs" into certain journalistic ears and the scandal hounds would be hot on the trail. "International athlete's sister a med student," "Access to performance-enhancing drugs." Suspicion would be quite enough to ruin a promising career.'

'So, our young genius was not averse to a spot of blackmail.'

'More than a spot, apparently. Sandra says that after his death she heard of two or three others Sutton was extracting money from. Not content with supplying them, he threatened to expose them unless they coughed up more cash.'

'Hence the glittering lifestyle.'

'So it seems. His sudden demise let several people off the hook.'

'Well, it was poetic justice that he OD'd on his own drugs.'

Jenny shook her head. 'Dr Cowley thinks not. She's sure he wasn't a user. He boasted to her that he was far too clever to fall into that trap. He said anyone taking hard drugs had to be either stupid or desperate – and he was neither.'

There was a thoughtful silence before Nat said, 'So Dr Cowley presumably believes that someone else was involved in Sutton's death.'

'She's convinced of it.'

'But she didn't go to the police with her suspicions?'

'No. Nor did anyone else in the know. They were scared of getting caught up in a purge of suspected drug-users. And, anyway, some of them, like Sandra Cowley, reckoned that justice had been well served by Sutton's murder.'

Nat scowled. 'Damn and blast! Now we are in a mess. Damn Zuylestein! Damn him! Damn him!'

'What's brought on that little outburst?' Kathryn asked brightly, coming in from the kitchen.

'I've been manoeuvred into an impossible position, that's what! Zuylestein wants me to throw open St Tom's cupboards so that all the world can see there are no skeletons in them. But as soon as we start ferreting around we discover a whole bloody graveyard of rattling bones.'

Kathryn perched on a corner of the table. 'Could you try being a little more coherent, Darling?'

Jenny said, 'Perhaps I'd better explain.' She gave Kathryn a brief résumé of her meeting with Sandra Cowley.

'Very nasty,' Kathryn said, 'but aren't you over-reacting a wee bit, Nat?'

'I don't think so. My brief from Zuylestein is to establish that two tragic accidents at St Tom's were just accidents. Nothing more sinister. No supernatural overtones. But what do we discover before we've been ten minutes on the case? Paul Sutton turns out to be not exactly the dedicated genius who only lived for his work and was cruelly cut down in his prime.'

Nat stood up and crossed to a corner cupboard. 'Anyone else for a drink?'

The women declined and Nat poured himself a brandy.

Kathryn said, 'That all happened a long time ago.'

'Huh! So what? You're a journalist. You know the scandal hounds will dig up old bones no matter how deep they're buried. And we have inadvertently helped them.'

'How so?'

'By stirring memories. There are at least four people who believe that Sutton was murdered: his parents, Sandra Cowley and the solicitor fellow – Tyrone. It won't be long before someone's talking to the press.'

'Ah, Tyrone, that reminds me.' Kathryn slipped into the chair Nat had vacated. 'Barny rang earlier. I didn't quite catch what he was on about. He was a bit excited. He said he had seen Tyrone and there was a photograph on his office wall of a college rowing eight – St Tom's.'

Nat let out a low whistle. 'Tyrone was at St Tom's? That could explain his interest in the Sutton case. What were Tyrone's university dates?'

'Barny said he was looking into that.'

Nat gulped down the cognac. 'This thing gets worse by the minute.'

Jenny looked up. 'Surely, it's not that bad. Old Zuylestein must realize that we could come up with information which wouldn't suit his book.'

'To tell the truth, it's not the revered Master of St Tom's that I'm really worried about.'

'What then?' Kathryn asked.

It was Jenny who answered. 'Has it got something to do with concealing a crime?'

'Bingo!' Nat nodded emphatically.

Jenny went on, 'I was thinking about that as I came back on the train. If we have reason to think that a crime has been committed shouldn't we go to the police?'

Kathryn protested. 'But you don't have reason to think a crime's been committed. It's just that a few people want to believe Paul Sutton was murdered. They don't have any proof. They're just using this "ghost" business to keep the story alive.'

Jenny said, 'Yes, but there may be something in this ghost business.'

Nat scowled. 'That's a secondary issue at the moment. If and when the papers and the police get wind of the latest developments, do you think we'll get away with keeping silent? The words "cover up" spring to mind. We could find ourselves accused of helping St Thomas's College to try to stop the truth coming out.'

There was a long silence, broken eventually by Jenny. 'Well, I guess I'd better be getting back.' She stood up. 'Thanks for the meal, Kathryn. Sorry to have landed on you without warning.'

Nat said, 'I'll run you back.'

'Oh, no you won't.' Kathryn pushed her chair back. 'Not unless you want to risk being breathalysed. I'll see that Jenny gets home in one piece. Besides, you have an appointment with two young men.' She pointed towards the stairs. 'A game of cards – remember?'

'Well, if you don't mind, Darling. That would be good. Oh, Jenny, one last thing: don't forget to email me your interview notes on the F5 hauntings?'

Jenny shrugged. 'Sure, but I don't think you'll find anything in them.'

'Just being thorough. Goodnight, Jenny. Thanks for coming.'

Later, as they were getting ready for bed, Kathryn asked, 'Have you calmed down now or are you still tormenting yourself dreaming up worst case scenarios?'

'I'm still wishing I'd never got mixed up in this St Tom's business. It's getting too damned complicated.'

Kathryn slipped between the sheets. 'It could be about to get more complicated.'

'Meaning?'

'There was another phone call today I didn't mention earlier. I thought you might blow your top.'

Nat slumped down on the edge of the bed. 'Go on, then, tell me. Things can't be much worse than they already are.'

'It was Celia Turner.'

Nat frowned. 'And who might Celia Turner be?'

'I'm not surprised you don't remember her. Timid little thing. She's married to Mike Turner. He's not much brighter. Junior fellow at St Tom's. Teaches history.'

'Ah yes. Now I can place them. We've met them a couple of times at concerts. She plays the flute, doesn't she? What did she want?'

'They're having what she called a non-New Year's Eve Party tomorrow evening and she's invited us.'

'What's a non-New Year's Eve Party?'

'What it sounds like, I imagine. The Turners, it seems, are not into ringing out the old and ringing in the new so they have a sort of musical soirée instead – on the penulti-mate evening of the year.'

'Bit late with their invites, aren't they, or have we been approached at the last minute to make up numbers?'

'Well, it *could* be that some other people have cried off.'

'Or?'

'Well, it's a bit of a coincidence, don't you think? The master tells you on no account to let the college fellows know what you're up to and a few days later one of the fellows we hardly know wants to pal up with us.'

'You reckon something's leaked out?'

'Don't you?'

'Very probably. Well, that does it! I spent this afternoon lying my way into the confidence of a perfectly decent couple. Jenny's discovered that their beloved son was a petty criminal. We're probably going to find ourselves in trouble with the police. And now, it seems, Zuylestein can't even keep the lid on things in the college. Time for me to bow out and distance myself as far as possible from this God-awful shambles.' He yanked his trousers off.

Kathryn stared up at him from the pillows. 'Jenny will be disappointed.'

Nat glared back. 'And that's another thing, you can stop this absurd jealous wife act. Jenny's an intelligent young

61

woman whose company I happen to enjoy. That's all there is to it – unless your ridiculous suspicions actually drive me to do something silly.'

Colour flared in Kathryn's cheeks but she assumed an air of calm. 'As a matter of fact I think Jenny is a nice kid. We had a chat in the car and . . .'

'Whatever it was, I don't want to hear about it!' Nat finished changing and jumped into bed.

It was a long time before either he or Kathryn fell asleep.

The Fifth Day of Christmas

Nat was up early. He fixed himself a strong coffee and sat at the kitchen table playing over in his mind the next – and final – scene in the F staircase melodrama. It was the scene in which he confronted the master and told him, politely but firmly, that he could not continue his investigation. He stared out of the window at the black tree skeletons slowly achieving sharp-etched outlines against a grey dawn and rehearsed the arguments that Zuylestein might produce. He imagined the old man's possible range of emotions from blustering anger to wheedling reproaches and planned appropriate responses. It was going to be an unpleasant interview but it had to be faced. Nat decided that he would call the master's lodge as soon as he decently could after breakfast.

The phone rang at 8.53. Nat answered it in the study.

'Is that Dr Gye?'

'Yes. Who's calling?'

'Gerald Sutton here. We met yesterday.'

The voice seemed strained and Nat said, 'Hello, Gerald. Is everything OK?'

'Well, no. Leastways *I'm* all right. It's the wife.'

'Oh, I'm sorry to hear that. What's the matter?'

'It's nothing serious . . . That's what they said . . . Just keeping her in for observation . . . A couple of days.'

'Mrs Sutton's in hospital? But why? She seemed fine yesterday.'

There was a long pause at the other end of the line, as

though Gerald was trying to assemble his thoughts. When the mental dam burst words came out in a rush.

'Look, Dr Gye, truth is, after you left we had a bit of an up and a downer. Jane wasn't best pleased that I'd shown you Paul's room. Said you might have got the wrong impression. I told her that if you were going to make a decent programme about our Paul you needed to know as much about him as possible. Then she got excited – hysterical really. Kept going on about "desecrating" Paul's memory. And . . . Well, the end of it was she collapsed.'

'Collapsed?'

'Yes, heart. She's got a bit of a history. I called the ambulance and we got her to A and E. By the time we were there she'd recovered pretty well but, like I say, they kept her in for tests and so on.'

'Well, Gerald, I'm very sorry to hear this. I assume you're phoning to tell me that you don't want to do the programme now. I quite understand. If Mrs Sutton's health isn't up to it . . .'

'Oh, no, Dr Gye, no. That isn't it at all. Quite the opposite in fact. Truth is, we can't go on like this, either of us. I can't tell you what the last ten years have been like. At first I thought the grieving would come to an end and the pain would be over. But Jane just refused to put it all behind us. Then, when all that ghost business started she convinced herself that Paul's spirit was trying to communicate. She got involved with a spiritualist church and I've lost count how many mediums she's consulted. So you see, Dr Gye, why I was over the moon when you got in touch about your programme. It's our one chance to close the book and make some sort of life in whatever years we've got left. So, I just wanted to say, you go right ahead. Full investigation. Everything out in the open. Lance the boil. There's a big word for it. What is it . . . "catharsis". Yes that's what we need, catharsis.'

Nat had made a couple of attempts to break in on Sutton's monologue. Now, he said, 'Gerald, I hear what you're saying but I must tell you that if we go ahead you may not like everything we turn up. One of my colleagues has been following a different line of enquiry and . . .'

'I suppose you mean the drugs.'

Nat gasped. 'You knew?'

There was silence at the other end of the line. Eventually Nat said, 'Gerald, hello! Are you still there?'

The reply was something between a croak and a groan. Then Sutton said in a voice heavy with misery, 'I suspected for some time that there must be something wrong. Paul always seemed to have money. He couldn't possibly have lived the way he did on what we were able to give him. Trips abroad, parties, and always new clothes – designer labels, of course. I worried that he was notching up a huge overdraft or borrowing from some rich kids at the university. Then, when he got himself that sports car, well, I knew he must be into something . . .'

Again the line fell silent but this time Nat let the other man take his time.

'One day, on one of Paul's rare visits home, I saw he'd gone out and left the key in the door to his room.'

'He kept his door locked?'

'Oh yes, had done for years. He called that room his secret kingdom. No one else was allowed in – he even cleaned it himself. Well, I had a snoop and in one of the drawers I found a little packet of white powder. It was a shock, I don't mind telling you. I couldn't believe it was . . . well . . . you know. So I took it to a friend of mine in the local CID. Said I'd found it in the front garden and thought someone must have dumped it there. He confirmed what I'd already suspected and feared.'

'Did you confront Paul?'

Gerald gave a half-laugh. 'I stopped confronting Paul when he was twelve. He'd fly into a rage if he thought anyone was against him.'

'Couldn't Jane have asked him about the drugs?'

'Oh, she just denied the whole thing. Convinced herself

that the police had made a mistake or that someone had planted heroin on Paul. Oh, no, he couldn't be mixed up in anything like that. Not her Paul. She's gone on pretending ever since and I haven't stopped her – more fool me.'

Nat floundered around for an adequate response. 'It's obviously been a terrible ordeal for you both. Surely, you don't want it all dragged up again – and made public through television.'

'The way I see it, if you shake the box something might fall out. There's no other way we're going to get close to what really happened to our son. Perhaps, just perhaps, we might get justice for him. What he was mixed up in was wrong, very wrong. But if someone killed him, well, there's nothing worse, is there, Dr Gye? With your help perhaps something will come out that the police can follow up.'

When the call ended Nat sat for a long time staring at the phone. The events of the previous day had depressed him but that was nothing compared to what he felt now. Why did everyone expect so much of him? Zuylestein, the Suttons; why was he the guru who was supposed to have an answer to their problems? No, it was too much. He would extricate himself from the quagmire before he got in any deeper. It would mean upsetting people but that was hardly his fault. Yes, he would inform the Master of St Tom's and the parents of Paul Sutton that he was no longer involved in their affairs.

But first he would have a quick word with Barny. The canny old lawyer always had a fresh and incisive way of looking at things. Nat picked up the handset again and punched in his friend's number.

'Good morning, Nathaniel.'

Nat jumped as Barny Cox's voice came not from the telephone but from the doorway behind him. He turned to see the slender, silver-haired and ever-immaculate lawyer smiling down at him and unnecessarily adjusting his bow-tie.

'My dear boy, I didn't mean to startle you. Kathryn told me to come straight up and who am I to disregard such a command? By the way I was to tell you that she's gone shopping with your sons.'

Nat waved him to the small room's other chair. 'Always glad to see you, Barny. As a matter of fact I was just in the process of phoning you. I've made a decision I must tell you about.'

Cox sat down, carefully pinching the creases in his trousers as he did so. 'I thought I should report back on yesterday's little foray since we're so short of time on this St Thomas's business.'

'I gather the Sutton's lawyer is a St Tom's man.'

Barny nodded. 'Not only that but an exact contemporary of Paul Sutton. He has a college rowing photo hanging on his office wall and that sent me back to the Law List to check his dates.'

'Interesting. Do you suppose he has his own motives for wanting to reopen old wounds?'

Barny pondered the question. 'He's the sort of man my grandmother used to describe as "so sharp he'll probably cut himself". I can't imagine him undertaking anything that wasn't to his own distinct advantage.'

'He certainly seems to have it in for his old college. And yet you say he was a member of a St Tom's eight.'

'That's right. First boat. But not only that; he was president of the boat club in his last year.'

'Not, on the face of it, someone disenchanted with his alma mater.'

Barny shrugged. 'One can never tell with young people nowadays. So full of angst. So *complicated*. Always putting their thoughts and feelings under the microscope. Time was when a man counted himself highly privileged to have a Cambridge education. Now some of them seem to think that they're bestowing an honour on the university by deigning to come here. As for Tyrone, if he has any residual affection for St Thomas's he won't let it get in the way of commercial gain.'

'So you think he *is* using the Suttons to prise some compensation out of the college?'

'That's the best working hypothesis I can produce at the moment.'

'Hmm, I wonder. It would be interesting to know what sort of a relationship he had with Paul Sutton.'

'Agreed. How do you intend to find that out? We can't ask Tyrone. That would let the cat out of the bag.'

'Jenny has unearthed someone who was involved in the Sutton circle during her undergraduate days.' Nat told Barny about the interview with Sandra Cowley.

'And the smarmy solicitor – what should we do about him?'

'Let him stew for a bit, I think. He might be more worried about a Law Society investigation than he's letting on. He'll find out soon enough from his clients that I'm involved and that could turn up the heat on him. It's still possible he might drop the Sutton case and that would pull all our chestnuts out of the fire.'

'I wouldn't bet your shirt on that eventuality, Nathaniel. He's just as likely to assume from all this interest that there really is something unsavoury to sniff out.'

Nat rubbed a weary hand over his eyes. 'God, Barny, this is a mess. We need something unexpected, some . . .'

'*Deus ex machina*?' Barny suggested.

'Deus, diabolus – anything to cast some light. At the moment all I can see is the whole business ending in tears – for all concerned.'

After the old lawyer had left, Nat turned back to the computer screen. He found the reports Jenny had emailed and printed them off. He skimmed through them and concluded that Jenny was probably right. They were brief and short on detail. Jenny had arranged them in date order and Nat saw that they fell into three groups. The first, and longest, recounted the experience of Sarah Belman (only now she elected to be known as Sarah Belman-Hicks), the undergraduate who had first reported alarming manifestations. Her testimony was supported by a friend and also by a Mrs Strang, the bedder responsible for cleaning F staircase. There then followed a gap of two years before anything untoward manifested itself again. At that time the occupant of F5 had been Rebecca Tan. After graduating she had returned to Hong Kong and Jenny had been unable to trace her but a group of the girl's friends had proved less elusive. It seemed fairly obvious that they had colluded to present a sensational story to the local press. After Rebecca had spoken excitedly of 'ghostly' noises, several of them had gathered in her room for 'psychic investigation', the main ingredients of which appeared to be a Ouijah board and a large quantity of beer. According to the highly coloured account they gave to the *Evening Star* they had ended up scaring the pants off each other. They reported hearing a disembodied male voice and seeing a hockey stick fly across the room.

A further couple of years passed without incident. The college had adopted the policy of allocating the top floor of F staircase to post-graduate students, presumably on the assumption that being older, they would also be wiser. Lydia Tasker must have been a disappointment to them. She had demanded to be moved because of 'intolerable nocturnal noises'. The forthright Ms Tasker declared herself to be no believer in 'supernatural nonsense', but she claimed to be the victim of 'architectural defects' which resulted in unacceptable creaking and bumping sounds. Methodical young woman that she was, Lydia had pre-pared a dossier for the bursar which included the testimony of two friends who had also heard the noises.

The final pair of interviewees were not members of St Thomas's or even of the university. Amy and Bill Stroat had turned up, uninvited, a couple of years previously and were, to all outward appearances, just two of the thousands of tourists who visit Cambridge every year and wander from college to college, guidebook in hand. But the Stroats had not come to gaze at medieval dining halls, Renaissance libraries or Gothic chapels. Mrs Stroat was a psychic medium. She and her husband had climbed straight to the second floor of F staircase in order to make contact with the troubled spirit.

Their quest had not been in vain. The redoubtable Amy had plonked herself on the top stair, swiftly entered into a trance and almost immediately made contact with the presence of a young man who was most anxious to communicate. The medium's faithful amanuensis had taken down the urgent message: 'They've got it wrong. Didn't kill myself.' 'Tell us what happened,' Bill Stroat had prompted. But, before the spirit had been able to respond, the séance had been brought to an abrupt end by the appearance of an under-porter, who had 'very high-handedly' demanded to know what was going on and had 'in a brusque manner' escorted the visitors out of the college. This brief encounter had been written up in *Beyond News*, the official organ of a network of spiritualist churches, and Jenny had quoted verbatim from this in compiling her report.

Nat made notes on all this material and had just begun entering them on his on-screen journal when Kathryn came in.

She stood behind him, hands on his shoulders. 'How's it going?' she enquired.

Nat précised Jenny's research.

'Doesn't sound very informative.'

'No. There's no real detail to go on. Odd about the timings, though.'

'How do you mean?'

'Well, there are long gaps in the supposed manifestations. Two years between Sarah Belman's experience and Rebecca Tan's. Then a similar gap before Lydia Tasker heard strange noises. And another year goes by before the Stroats' encounter.'

Kathryn slumped into the chair beside the desk. 'God, I hate shopping, especially with two kids in tow, over-endowed with Christmas money to spend. Is that a problem?'

Nat stared at the lines of print on the screen. 'We can't very well stop relatives spoiling them.'

Kathryn looked puzzled. 'What? No, I mean your periodic ghost. Isn't it just a question of some people being more susceptible than others – psychic, I mean?'

'Oh, sure – psychic or psychiatrically disposed. It's just that when a place gets a reputation for being haunted it's almost impossible to shake it off. A kind of built-in expectancy occurs. People claim strange encounters – even when there are perfectly rational explanations for them.'

'Well, perhaps your ghost has better things to do than hang around his old college all the time.' Kathryn hauled herself out of the chair. 'Anyway, I must get on. There's a mountain of pre-Christmas emails that need answering.' She paused in the doorway. 'By the way, if we're going to the Turners' soirée, remember it's black tie.'

The Turners' party was a select affair, which further confirmed Nat's suspicion that theirs had been a last-minute invitation. A dozen or so fellow academics, most of them with their partners, made up the company which scattered itself around St Thomas's Long Room, a Jacobethan chamber of oak-panelled walls and moulded ceilings. Chairs had been set in short rows lengthwise to face a performing area beneath a group portrait – 'School of Vandyke' – depicting a reclining aristocratic family in the last stages of terminal ennui. From this stage a succession of Celia Turner's friends regaled the company with items from Schubert lieder to a Bartok bagatelle. After an hour an interval was announced for guests to help themselves to food and wine at the far end of the room. It was while Nat was selecting *bouchées* of smoked salmon and deep-fried camembert that Mike Turner sidled up to him.

'Nat, so glad you could make it.' The host offered a wan smile that failed to conceal a suggestion of anxiety.

Nat watched him load items of food haphazardly on to his plate. 'Lovely party,' he responded dutifully. 'Thank you for inviting us.' He turned to face the room. If Turner had something to say he could make the running. As he moved

71

back to the seated area the younger man stayed beside him. When Nat sat down Turner occupied the next chair.

'So, when's your next TV appearance?' he asked brightly.

'Still in the research stage, at the moment. I think they're hoping to film early next year.'

'Is one allowed to enquire the subject?'

Nat sipped his glass of pleasant merlot appreciatively. 'Oh, it'll be very much the mixture as before. People send in their stories of hauntings; our researchers follow them up and we choose the more interesting examples.' Nat concentrated ostentatiously on his food and waited for Turner to steer the conversation towards the F5 problem.

'It must take a lot of time. Do you find it interferes with your academic work? I mean, do your colleagues take you less seriously?'

Nat laughed. 'The green dragons in their ivory towers? Oh yes, every discipline has its anti-dumbing-down brigade who conceal their jealousy behind a veil of academic purity. Mustn't let the vulgar public into the sacred groves of academe.'

'You sound a little bitter.' Turner peered at him through thick-lensed glasses.

'I would be if I thought it mattered. I had to weigh up the pros and cons carefully before I decided to take the media man's shilling.'

'No regrets?'

'Quite the contrary. Television exposure has brought me more contacts than I could ever have imagined. People with stories and experiences I'd never have come across in the normal line of research. Purists who think that all I'm doing is simplifying or sensationalizing psychology for the plebs have no idea. It's a two-way street. I'm learning all the time.'

'Really? That's very interesting.' Turner's food remained untouched. 'So you'd recommend TV punditry?'

'It's not right for everyone. You have to be the sort of person who can stand up to producers and editors. I had a hell of a fight over my first series. It very quickly dawned on me that what my new masters wanted was M.R. James and Edgar Allan Poe in modern dress. Took a couple of very heated script conferences before I got my own way – or almost my own way.'

Turner prodded absentmindedly with his fork at something colourful trapped in a cube of aspic. 'Look, Nat,' he said after an agonized silence, 'I've got a confession to make. I had an ulterior motive in getting Celia to invite you this evening.'

The Sixth Day of Christmas

'Well?' As their car cleared the last of the town traffic, Kathryn cast a quizzical sideways glance at her husband.

'Well what?' Nat peered past the waving windscreen wipers into the headlight beam.

'Oh, don't be coy. You know what I mean. You and Mike Turner were locked in long and earnest debate. Was he probing your interest in the St Tom's ghost?'

Nat chuckled. 'No, as a matter of fact his concern was much more with *this* world.'

'Meaning?'

'He wants me to use my supposed influence to get him on to the telly.'

Kathryn laughed. 'My God! What happened to scholarship being its own reward?'

'Terminally ill; if not already defunct.' He turned the Mercedes off the Grantchester road and took the smaller, more direct route to Great Maddisham. 'I suppose that's not altogether fair. Our host did put up a token fight with his conscience. He wanted me to reassure him that it's OK to prostitute one's intellect.'

'Can you do anything for him?'

'Probably not. I traded him a couple of phone numbers.'

'Traded?'

'Mmm. It seemed too good an opportunity to miss, so I asked if he could get me a discreet look at F staircase.'

'Wasn't that a bit risky? I mean, won't he smell a rat?'

'Very probably but, frankly, I'm past caring. All this

secrecy is getting out of hand. If Zuylestein wants my help, I'm not going to give it with one hand tied behind my back.'

'So you're off to St Tom's for a midnight vigil, are you?'

'Nothing so dramatic. I've arranged for Mike to let me into the supposedly haunted room tomorrow evening.'

'New Year's Eve?'

'Yes, we're not partying, so it's an ideal time. Most fellows in residence will be off carousing somewhere. I should be able to have a good old snoop well away from prying eyes.'

'What do you expect to discover?'

'Probably nothing. Jenny's pretty convinced that Hockridge saw something on the upper stair that startled him. If that's so then whatever it was is likely to have been corporeal. If there *was* someone there, playing silly buggers, it should be possible to work out how that someone got there – and got away again without being seen.'

'That sounds logical. Won't the police have fine-tooth-combed the place?'

'Shouldn't think so. Hockridge died of a heart attack following a fall. The circumstances may have been bizarre but the coroner was satisfied. The police would be delighted not to be involved.'

'But if you can prove that someone else *was* skulking on the staircase, won't they have to investigate?'

Nat slowed to let an oncoming car pass in the narrow lane. 'Not my problem. I report to Zuylestein. What he does with the information is up to him.'

'You're getting callous in your old age.'

Nat shrugged. 'You know how I feel about this whole bloody business.'

Kathryn scowled. 'And I suppose you're still blaming me for getting you involved.'

'No, of course not, Darling. It was just an unhappy chapter of accidents. Anyway,' he turned to smile at her, 'I've worked out a suitable penance for you.'

'Oh?'

'You can come to St Tom's with me. Fancy a bit of sleuthing by torchlight?'

'Sorry, no can do.'

'What do you mean?'

'I'm going into the office tomorrow. I told you.'

'You never did.' Nat slowed to turn the car on to their drive. 'What's the point of going in on New Year's Eve? No one else will be there.'

'That's precisely the point. I'll have complete peace and quiet. I need to clear my desk. We've got three big features to do for our spring numbers. Don't you ever listen to what I say?' Kathryn grimaced as she struggled to unhitch her seat-belt.

'So, who's looking after the boys? Suzanne's not due back till the end of the week.'

'You are, my sweet. All life doesn't revolve round au pairs.' She stepped out of the car and went to open the garage door.

By the time Nat had driven in and switched off the engine he was fuming. As Kathryn opened the door to the house he grabbed her arm. 'It might be nice if you occasionally discussed your plans with me,' he hissed.

'Look who's talking.'

Nat maintained his grip. 'My God, Kathryn, what's come over you? You're getting so . . . so bloody . . .'

She put a finger to her lips and stepped across the threshold. '*Pas devant la baby-sitter*, my dear.'

It was eight o'clock the next evening that Nat drove the car into the fellows' car park at Beaufort College. He emerged into Silver Street and walked along to the main entrance. Jenny was waiting by the massive oak doors.

'This is all very exciting,' she said, as she went up to him. 'How did you manage it?'

'Let's just call it an exchange of favours. Have you brought a strong torch with you?'

She brandished a very professional-looking piece of

equipment. 'My landlord's a plumber. I believe he uses this for inspecting drains.'

'Excellent. I've got one, too. Not such an industrial model, but it will serve. Let's go.'

As they walked along King's Parade, Jenny asked, 'Why do we need torches? Can't we switch the lights on when we get there?'

'Two reasons, really. One is, I want to recreate something of the atmosphere of your last visit. It might help you to remember some little detail you could have overlooked. The other reason is so that we attract as little attention as possible. Lights on in rooms that are supposed to be un-occupied might lead to some awkward questions being asked.'

They walked some minutes in silence and were halfway along Trinity Street before Jenny said hesitantly, 'Nat, may I ask you something . . . personal?'

'Depends how personal, I suppose.'

'Well, it's none of my business but, well, is everything OK between you and Kathryn?'

Nat stared down at the elfin-like face under its woolly hat. 'Why on earth shouldn't it be?'

'I don't know. Just a feeling I had the other evening.'

Opposite St John's they turned into All Saints' Passage. Nat considered his reply carefully. He said nonchalantly, 'All marriages – all relationships – have their good and bad days. Just a case of post-Christmas blues, I think. Don't give it another thought.'

'OK.' Jenny suddenly linked her arm through his. 'It's just that, if anything was wrong I'd hate it to have anything to do with me.'

At St Thomas's they went to Dr Turner's rooms and found, as arranged, an envelope pinned to his outer door. Nat opened it and read the note inside.

Dear Nat. Very many thanks in anticipation for your help. Sorry I can't be here to accompany you but I'm sure you can pick up the vibes – or whatever it is you want to do – without me. Just put the key back here when you've finished. Happy hunting.

Yours sincerely, Mike

The courtyard was deserted as Nat and Jenny skirted the wet grass and entered the unlit staircase in the far corner. Nat switched on his torch and they climbed to the first landing. He shone the beam round the small space.

'So this is where it all happened.'

'Yes.' Jenny pointed to the college servants' room. 'Andy set up his equipment in there. Little Cynth and I were hovering here.'

'And when Hockridge arrived he went blustering straight up there?' Nat flashed his torchlight up the second flight of stairs.

'Yes, he . . .' Jenny shivered. She cleared her throat. 'Sorry . . . it's all coming back pretty vividly. Hockridge had just turned the bend, there. Then he screamed and threw his arms up. The next thing . . .'

'Just a minute, Jenny.' Nat put a hand on her arm. 'Let's take this in slow motion. You say the professor had gone round the bend, out of sight. So, how could you see him put his arms up?'

'Well . . .' Jenny screwed her face in a confused frown. 'It was all so quick. I know he turned the corner and he was still going up. But I know I saw him try to fend something off.'

'Perhaps he stepped back.'

'Y. . .e. . .s.' Jenny hesitated. 'I suppose . . . Yes, that must have been it, mustn't it?'

'I don't want to put ideas in your head. If you're not completely happy with that explanation, say so and we'll see if we can work out something that fits better.'

Jenny shook her head vigorously. 'No, that must be it. Anyway, it doesn't much matter, does it? I mean, the pompous idiot blustered up there, met something that gave him a nasty shock and . . . ended up here.' She pointed to the bottom stair.

'And nothing on Andy's state-of-the-art equipment?'

'So he says.'

'Hmm, I think I'd like to check that out for myself. Anyway, shall we go on up?'

There were just two doors off the next landing. One, facing the stairs, turned out to be a bathroom. F5 was to the right.

Nat asked, 'Why only one student room on this level? There are two on each of the others.'

'Through there,' Jenny pointed to the blank wall on the left, 'is the Fellows' Drawing Room. Very nice. I was invited in there by the bursar when he laid out the ground rules for our investigation.'

Nat now opened the door to F5. He shone his torch inside. 'Yes, you're absolutely right about this place. Quite a lumber room.'

When Jenny had switched on her torch the two beams probed a room some five metres by four filled almost to head height with piled stacking chairs, tables and desks atop one another and rolled carpets. Jenny stepped forward but Nat laid a restraining hand on her shoulder.

'Go carefully. We're looking for signs of activity.'

Jenny played her beam over flat furniture surfaces. 'Well, the dust doesn't seem to have been disturbed. This lot obviously hasn't been moved for months.'

Nat closed the door behind him. 'What about the floor?'

Jenny knelt down and tested the bare boards with her fingers. 'This won't tell us much,' she said, rising and wiping her hand on the sleeve of her anorak. 'The police were clumping about in here on the evening of the,' she hesitated, 'accident, if that's what it was.'

'Yes, of course. I'd forgotten the boys in blue with their size fifteens.'

There was an aisle between the lumber and the left-hand wall which housed a boarded-in fireplace. Nat advanced cautiously.

80

'Before these were turned into bedsits, they must have been pretty cosy. Can't you just imagine the sons of the gentry lolling by the fire, puffing their cigars while some lackey toasted their muffins and crumpets? Hello, what's this?'

He had crunched something underfoot. Shining the torch downwards he saw some tiny fragments of glass.

'Now, how did that get there?'

'Presumably, from the picture on the mantelpiece,' Jenny suggested.

Together they scrutinized a framed nineteenth-century engraving of Great Court, Trinity, minus its glass.

'Someone must have knocked it over,' Jenny said.

'OK,' Nat mused, 'but where's the glass?'

'You've just trodden in it.'

Nat shook his head. 'No, I've just trodden in *some* of the glass – to be precise, one piece of it. Look.' He shone the torch on the fragments. 'There's only a few square centimetres here. Where's the rest?'

'Tidied up, I suppose.'

'Uhu! Who by?'

'College staff, presumably. They must come here to take things out from time to time.'

'I suppose that's the most obvious answer. And yet . . .' He rubbed a finger along his nose.

'Yes, what, Nat?'

'Well, wouldn't a college cleaner have done an efficient, dustpan-and-brush job? Would she have missed one obvious bit of glass?'

'What's the alternative?'

'Someone moving about in the dark or by torchlight, as we are, brushes against the picture and knocks it off. What does he do? He puts it back on the mantelpiece and gathers up the glass fragments as best he can. Easy enough to miss one.'

'Isn't that a bit far-fetched?'

'Absolutely.' Nat gave a cynical half-laugh. 'About as

81

far-fetched as people hearing supposedly ghostly noises coming from this room. As far-fetched as someone appearing on that landing, scaring the wits out of Hockridge and, then, disappearing into thin air.'

'I see what you mean. So are we looking for a way in and out of this room without using the door?'

'Well, if there isn't at least somewhere for a flesh-and-blood person to hide, the only alternative must be . . .'

'Yes, I see.' Jenny instinctively moved closer to him.

'Well,' Nat said, 'if the spirit of Paul Sutton is hovering around here, let's hope he realizes we're on his side. Now,' he added briskly, 'let's not waste time. Do you think you could squeeze your petite frame between those chairs over there and see if there's anything along that wall at the end – a window seat, or cupboard, or even a chest of some sort where a man could hide?'

While Jenny burrowed through the stacked furniture Nat turned his attention to the fireplace wall. The area each side of the chimney breast had been filled in. To the right there were floor-to-ceiling bookshelves; to the left a cupboard. When he tugged at its door it yielded with some reluctance. The space was almost filled by another pile of stacking chairs. There was no room for anyone to conceal himself and, he reasoned, in any case it would be the first place the police would have looked. He explored the fireplace but the board covering it was well screwed into place and had clearly not been disturbed in decades. The bookshelves, similarly, yielded nothing of interest. They ran the full depth of the embrasure. There was no suggestion of the modern equivalent of a priest-hole.

Jenny sidled out from among the pillars of furniture. 'Nothing over there,' she reported. 'How are you getting on?'

'I've drawn a blank, too.' He perched on the edge of a desk. 'It's maddening!'

Jenny said, 'You don't want to believe in the psychic manifestation alternative, do you?'

'On the contrary, my mind is wide open to that explanation but you know the statistics as well as I do. Eighty-seven and a half per cent of all mysterious happenings, whether aural or visual, turn out to have explanations which anchor them firmly to this world.'

'Well, it looks as though this case belongs in the other twelve and a half per cent. I mean, poltergeist activity could account for the broken picture.'

'Have you ever come across a mischievous spirit that tidied up after itself?'

'Well, no, but . . .'

'I'm just sure that someone has been in here.'

'Making repeated visits over several years?'

Nat shrugged. 'Who knows? I agree my hypothesis doesn't make a great deal of sense but it does fit the few facts we've got. If only we could prove it.' He turned towards the door. 'Oh well, there's no point in hanging around here. Come on. A warming drink is called for.'

'You can say that again.'

They left F5 and Nat locked the door behind them.

'Lovely night,' Jenny said as they emerged into the court. The air was frosty and the ebonized sky above speckled with stars that seemed particularly brilliant. 'Shame we live in a city,' she went on. 'We could see even more clearly if it weren't for the man-made glare. The street lights make a real barrier. I was reading somewhere the other day just how much we miss . . .' She was suddenly aware that she was talking to herself. Turning, she saw Nat striding back towards F staircase.

By the time she had caught up with him he was at the door of F5 and turning the key in the lock.

'Forgotten something?' she asked.

'More like remembered,' he said.

He stepped across to the cupboard by the fireplace and yanked the door open. He shone his torch on the stack of chairs.

'I wonder. I just wonder. Come here, and I'll give you a leg-up.'

'What?'

'I want you to stand on top of these chairs.'

'What on earth . . . They look a bit precarious.'

'You'll be OK. Come on!' He cupped his hands.

Diffidently, Jenny allowed herself to be hoisted upwards. The chairs swayed ominously but she managed to scramble on top. She knelt there looking down quizzically. 'Now what?'

'Stand up. Can you reach the ceiling?'

'Yes.'

Nat shone the torch on the bare boards above her head. 'Try pushing those planks. See if anything moves.'

Balancing herself gingerly and clinging with one hand to the chair back, Jenny lifted the other to the ceiling about thirty centimetres above her head.

'No,' she muttered. 'It all seems pretty firm. Ouch!' She coughed and spluttered, as a shower of dust suddenly descended. She rubbed her eyes. 'Something gave,' she said.

'I knew it! See if you can push the plank there aside.'

Seconds later Jenny had moved two of the broad ceiling boards to make a hole almost a metre wide.

Nat handed up one of the torches. 'What's up there, Jenny?'

She directed the beam through the opening. 'Loft space. Lots of dust. And probably bats, I shouldn't wonder.'

'Up you go, then.'

Jenny hauled herself up and sat perched on the edge of the hole, still brushing dust from her face.

'Right,' Nat said, 'give me a hand. I'm coming up.'

He collected another chair and, by standing on it, managed to move himself to the top of the stack. Jenny helped him into the loft. They stood, flashing their torches round the sixteenth-century rafters and cross beams.

'This obviously runs the whole length of the building,' Nat said. 'There are three chimney stacks coming up through, apart from this one.'

'Is that significant?'

'You bet.' Nat spoke excitedly. 'What goes up must come down. Let's have a look. But quietly. We don't want to announce our presence.'

They crossed carefully to the next chimney and explored the timbers around it. They were all very firmly in place and showed no signs of being disturbed. The second chimney was different. Two of the boards to one side were raised slightly above the level of their neighbours. Nat inserted a penknife along one edge and the plank yielded.

'Can you see anything?' he whispered.

Jenny knelt and shone her torch through the aperture. 'No, just a dark space.' Then, excitedly, 'Hang on a minute. There's a ladder. Want me to go down?'

'Better not. All we need to know is what room it's in.'

'That's easy,' Jenny replied, standing up. 'It's the Fellows' Drawing Room. It has two fireplaces with cupboards between. This must be the one nearest the door.'

'Really?' Nat eased the prised board quietly back into place. 'Then the plot, as they say, thickens.'

Twenty minutes later they were seated in the corner of a crowded city centre bar struggling to hold a conversation against the noise of a large party of revellers.

'Ah, that's welcome,' Jenny gasped, taking a long draught of lager. 'My throat's still full of dust. Whatever made you think of looking for the hidden entrance in the cupboard?'

Nat set down his glass of Greene King. 'Crossing neuro-circuits in the brain, I guess. Something in the unconscious questioned why anyone would put a stack of chairs *inside* the cupboard but it didn't surface until you talked about the night sky.'

'You've lost me.'

Nat laughed. 'I've probably lost myself. I think it must have been something to do with reaching for the stars. It suddenly occurred to me that someone might pile the chairs up if they were reaching for something.'

Jenny grinned. 'No wonder people accuse psychologists of having twisted minds. Anyway, now we know that someone came out of F5 and gave old Hockridge a hell of a fright.'

'Correction: we know that someone was in the habit of making secret visits to F5 and that someone *might* have appeared to Hockridge.'

'No, I'm convinced, now, that we've found the answer to the old boy's sudden shock. It must—'

Nat interrupted. 'Maybe, but don't you see that that's not the most important point. We've narrowed the search for whoever is behind all the chaos on F staircase.'

'It must be one of the senior members?'

'They're the only people who have access to the Fellows' Drawing Room. I reckon we can discount college staff.'

'So you think one of the fellows has been systematically fabricating the supposed hauntings? Surely, that's a bit far-fetched. I mean, think of all the harm it's done St Tom's. He'd have to be mad to carry on such a vicious joke for so long.'

Nat smiled ruefully. 'It has been observed on more than one occasion that insanity is a required qualification for election to a Cambridge fellowship.' After another mouth-ful of bitter he added, 'I wonder what Zuylestein knows or suspects.'

'You think he's on to something?'

'He was adamant that I shouldn't breathe a word to any of his colleagues.'

Jenny sat back with a frown of concentration and Nat noticed the way her nose wrinkled like that of a bemused child. 'So what have we got?' she asked. 'A vindictive little bastard by the name of Paul Sutton who puts his un-doubted brilliance to work ruining the lives of other people. He does very nicely out of drug-running, not to mention a lucrative sideline in blackmail. He gets what he richly deserves – either by accident or at the hands of one of his victims. Then, mysterious events start happening in the room where his body was found and some people believe that it's haunted – which, of course, may be true,' she added hurriedly.

Nat nodded. 'That's more or less right.'

'But now we're saying that some senior member of the college deliberately played on this rumour by sneaking into F5 to scare people with ghostly noises. He does his job so well that now one of his own colleagues is dead. This is just bizarre.'

Nat nodded. 'Totally bizarre. And we mustn't forget Sutton's contemporary, Tyrone. He's also trying to keep the story alive.'

Jenny sat back in her bench seat and closed her eyes. She pulled off the woolly hat and her short, dark hair reflected the flashing, festive lights draped round the window. 'It's all tied up with something pretty murky that was happening in St Tom's ten years ago.'

'Yes. And one thing that's been intriguing me is the financial angle. For an undergrad from a modest background Sutton was seriously rich. No horrendous overdraft; no holiday jobs to eke out his scholarship. He's into smart cars and parties and frequent travel.'

'Drug-dealing pays well.'

'Yes, but only to those near the top of the tree. You know the sort of sums a student pusher can get selling on small quantities to his friends. Sutton must have been in the trade at a fairly high level.'

'Got it!' Jenny opened her eyes wide and sat forward. 'Supposing one of the St Tom's fellows was the Mr Big. Paul and the Tyrone guy were his lieutenants. Then, there was a falling-out – perhaps because Paul was getting greedy. So Mr Big decided to get rid of him.'

Nat smiled. 'OK so far but what about all the subsequent activity?'

'Well that's obvious,' Jenny went on triumphantly. 'Paul was too smart not to have some kind of insurance policy. He had a penchant for blackmail. He was in a position to

87

destroy Mr Big's academic career and put him behind bars. He kept his own business notes hidden in his rooms somewhere. Mr Big's been looking for them ever since and doing his best to make sure F5 remains empty.'

Nat laughed. 'Brilliant, my dear Watson! That would make a very good storyline for a TV whodunit.'

Jenny grinned, unoffended. 'Well my dear Holmes, what was it you once said – "When you've eliminated the impossible, whatever remains, however improbable, must be the truth."' She looked suddenly at her watch. 'Hey, ten fifteen! I must go. Some friends in King's are having a party and I promised I'd look in. She crammed her hat on and zipped up her anorak. 'Why don't you come along? I don't like to think of you seeing the New Year in all by yourself.'

Nat finished his drink and set down the glass. 'Thanks, Jenny, but I don't think I'd cut much of a dash among your young friends.' He led the way through the crush to the door.

Outside, the keen frosty air almost took their breath away.

Jenny said, 'Oh, don't be such a fuddy-duddy. I know they'd all love to meet *the* Nathaniel Gye.'

Nat laughed. 'That gives me an even better reason to avoid them.'

They parted company outside King's College and Nat collected his car from Beaufort. Back in Great Maddisham he discovered Tracy, the sixteen-year-old baby-sitter, curled up on the sofa watching television. She reported that the boys were 'well asleep'.

'Good,' he said, 'and thanks for coming in at such short notice. I hope I haven't kept you from a party.'

'That's OK,' she said. 'Partying's off till after the exams.' She indicated a pile of textbooks on the floor beside her. 'Oh, by the way, Mrs Gye phoned. She said she'd be home about midday tomorrow. She's staying in the office flat overnight.'

'Fine, I'll just ring her back while you get your things together. Then I'll run you home.'

In the study he phoned Kathryn's office. After a few rings there was a click and the call was diverted to another terminal. A man's voice said, 'Hello, Styline House.'

'Hello. I was trying to reach Mrs Gye in the *Panache* Suite. Who am I speaking to?'

'This is office security, sir. All calls are routed here when the building's empty.'

'I see. This is Mrs Gye's husband. My wife has been working in her office all day and she is planning to stay over in the *Panache* flat. Could you try the extension there, please?'

'There's no one in here, sir. Been quiet as the tomb all day – or anyway, since I came on at two o'clock.'

'No, there must be some mistake. Mrs Gye is there. She phoned home from there this evening.'

'Sorry, sir. We do our rounds every hour. She hasn't been in – not unless she was hiding behind the filing cabinet?' He laughed at his own joke.

Nat felt a sudden tightening of his chest. He said, 'OK, my mistake. Sorry to trouble you. Goodnight.'

'Goodnight, sir. And a happy New Year to you.'

Nat descended the stairs thoughtfully. At the bottom he said, 'Tracy, do you think your parents would mind if I asked you to stay another couple of hours? I find I have to go out again.'

She smiled. 'That'll be OK, Dr Gye. If you explain.'

Nat ordered a taxi to take him to King's College.

The Seventh Day of Christmas

Hangovers and energetic small boys do not go together.

Nat made this discovery slowly and painfully during his first waking hours of the new year. Jerry had appointed himself breakfast cook and spent half an hour rattling and banging pans, plates and dishes around the kitchen. Nat strove manfully to maintain a pose of cheerful gratitude by eating the overdone food set before him, though his head and stomach were united in rebellion. They were only reluctantly appeased by two mugs of black coffee. When the dishwasher had been stacked he tried to palm off his sons with a PlayStation game but they clamoured for him to come and 'play ball' so that they could practise with their baseball gloves. Somehow Nat found the energy to do the fatherly thing for half an hour in the garden and gradually the crisp winter air cleared his head. After a while, the boys' voices seemed less shrill and the world became a normal and familiar place.

But then memory kicked in – and kicked was the right word. The previous night's party was still, mercifully, something of a blur. There had been flashing lights, cacophonous music, people contorting themselves in primal response to the unremitting thud of the drums, and shouted attempts at conversation which Nat had quickly abandoned. He recalled retreating into a corner with a glass – the first of several obligingly refilled by his hosts. At midnight, everything had peaked in cheers, hugs and kisses. Beyond that the sequence of events was vague. What he did remember with sickening clarity was Kathryn's deception. She had lied about her day and night in London and he could think of only one reason why she would do that.

An hour later, when the boys had gone off to play with friends on the other side of the green, he sat listlessly in front of his computer console. What to do? Have it out? Confront Kathryn as soon as possible and discuss the situation 'calmly and rationally'. He felt anything but calm and rational. Pretend ignorance, then? Say nothing. Leave the initiative to Kathryn and hope that her conscience . . .

The screen before him filled with words. While disjointed thoughts jangled in his brain his fingers had tapped the keys which brought up his journal. Now he keyed in 'St Thomas's College' and allowed his mind to escape into a different problem. Recalling and setting down the details of his clandestine visit to F5 was a valuable mental exercise. Having recorded the facts, he tried to draw some logical conclusions:

> Can we really believe that one of St Tom's seniors has set up an elaborate and uncomfortable method for getting into F5?
>
> It would be useful to check the cupboard in the Fellows' Drawing Room. Zuylestein will be able to arrange that.
>
> If the answer to the last question is 'Yes', then why?
> Eccentricity?
> Hardly.
> Searching for something?

Nat summarized Jenny's theory of a drug-dealing senior academic seeking out incriminating evidence.

> Far-fetched but worth testing. Which of today's fellows were around ten years ago? Did any of them have connections with Sutton?

It was easy to answer the first question. The on-line University Register provided Nat with the names of ten St

Tom's fellows who had been continually in residence for the past ten years. Nat went through the list. One could, presumably, remove the dean's name. Then there were four dons well advanced in years whom one could not imagine climbing precariously into a dusty attic. Nat noted the remaining names in the journal:

Sumpter, R.A., PhD (Molecular Biology)
Manton, P. de B., Q, PhD (English)
Sanderson, Professor D.J., MB, BChir., MD
   (Medical Sciences)
Grimm, S.P., PhD (Mathematics) (Bursar)
Philigrew, T.N.J., PhD (History) (Senior Tutor)
Can we cut the list down any further?

He phoned Barny and, after only a couple of rings, the old lawyer's brisk voice answered. Nat summarized the events of the previous evening, then read over the shortlist of potential criminals he had just drawn up.

'Dear boy, what an exciting life you do lead. I must say the mind boggles at what young Jenny has suggested. Distinguished colleagues consorting with the criminal underworld? Surely not. Mind you,' he paused, 'there was a case back in the late seventies of serious financial fraud. Mathematician at Emmanuel, I think, or it may have been Downing, gathered a little coterie of bright students and devised a system for cheating the gambling casinos.'

'Very interesting, Barny, but do you know these St Tom's fellows? Can you vouch for any of them?'

'Of course there's a world of moral difference between financial chicanery and heroin trafficking. St Thomas's fellows? Give me the names again, would you, Nathaniel?'

Nat patiently recited the list.

'No, can't say that I know them. I've met a couple of them but that's not to say I could provide them with character references.'

'Thanks, Barny, I was just calling on the off chance.'

'Of course, you can strike Dr Manton off your list.'

'Oh, why's that?'

'Poor fellow's a cripple, though I suppose we're not allowed to use that word today – non-PC. Better say he's handicapped, physically impaired. Skiing accident, I believe. He has an artificial lower leg. He gets around very well but walks with a stick. I can't imagine him climbing into attics.'

'Thank you, Barny, that's very helpful.'

'My pleasure, dear boy. But that still leaves four names on your list. How do you propose to whittle it down further?'

'I don't know. There's not much point in asking Zuylestein. He's only been in Cambridge a few months. He won't really know his senior members very well. You couldn't make discreet enquiries among some of your old cronies, could you? See if there's ever been any hint of scandal attached to one or other of our suspects?'

'I can and I will. Any other way I can help?'

Nat thought a moment. 'Perhaps it's time we leaned more heavily on friend Tyrone.'

'A nice thought. He should be back in his office tomorrow. I'll give him a call and suggest another meeting.'

'Excellent, Barny. Keep me posted. Goodbye for now.'

Nat had scarcely put the phone down when it rang. It was Jenny. 'Hi, Nat, how are you feeling?'

'Better than I felt a couple of hours ago. How about you?'

'I'm OK.'

'I was on the point of calling to thank you for last night.'

'You got home all right, then?'

'Yes . . . er . . . did I . . .?'

'No, not at all!' Jenny laughed. 'I made sure we got you into a taxi before things got that far.'

'Yes, I vaguely remember. I was compos mentis enough to put the baby-sitter in the same cab and send her home. Still, it's all very embarrassing.'

'It wasn't at all embarrassing. Everyone was very relaxed. I was delighted you were able to let your hair down.'

'As long as I didn't let it down too far.'

'No. Your reputation is quite safe. Anyway, what's the next move on the St Tom's business?'

Nat explained how he had whittled down the number of fellows who could have used the concealed entrance to F5.

'Well, my money's on the bursar,' Jenny promptly replied.

'Why's that?'

'Grimm by name and grim by nature. He's a surly beggar and he very definitely didn't want my unit going anywhere near the place. When he showed me the room he barely let me get my nose inside the door. It was, "There you are, Miss Collard, as I told you, chock full of spare furniture." Slam! And of course he's the one who made sure that F5 was put permanently out of use.'

'That's true. We must see what we can find out about him. Meanwhile, do you think you can set up a meeting with Andy Rowsell? I'd like to see whether he can add anything to the events surrounding Hockridge's death. Do you know whether he's in Cambridge at the moment?'

'I expect so. He lives with a nurse from Addenbrooke's. If he's not off on one of his fishing trips, he'll be at home – not that you'll get much out of him. Not the most communicative of men, our Andy.'

Nat's next call was to the Master of St Thomas's.

'Dr Gye, good, good. I was hoping I might hear from you soon.' Nat could hear the relief in Zuylestein's voice. 'What have you got to report?'

Nat replied cautiously. 'I'm still sifting the information I've gathered, Sir Joseph. I've just called to ask if there's something you can help me with.'

'Of course, of course. Why don't you come to the lodge for lunch and we can discuss progress to date?'

'That's very kind of you, Sir Joseph, but I think it would be better to wait till I have something concrete for you. What I was wondering was whether I might have a quick, discreet look at the Fellows' Drawing Room.'

'Fellows' Drawing Room? What on earth . . .? No, I suppose I'd better not ask. I'm sure you have your reasons. Certainly. When do you want to come?'

'As soon as possible. I assume there aren't many people around today.'

'Indeed, indeed. Most of the resident fellows are away. There may be a couple lunching in the Small Parlour. We mostly use that for meals in vacation time. In fact, lunch would be a good time to find the Drawing Room empty. Shall we say one-ish? Come to the lodge. It connects directly with the north side of Old Court, so we shan't be observed.'

'Pathetic secrecy!' Nat muttered as he returned the handset to its pod. How long does he think he can get away with it? Nat recalled the words of Benjamin Franklin, 'Three may keep a secret, if two of them are dead.'

'Hello! I'm home!' Kathryn's bright voice called from the foot of the stairs.

Nat felt something akin to a heavy punch in the solar plexus. He stood up, checked the contents of his briefcase and, tucking it under his arm, moved to the door. Kathryn was half-sitting, half-lying on the sofa. She looked tired. Not much sleep, probably, Nat thought. She stretched her arms.

'Good to be back,' she said.

Nat headed straight for the side door. 'I'm glad,' he said. 'See you later. By the way, the boys are over at Michael's. Bye!' He went into the garage, seated himself in the Mercedes and drove out quickly.

After a pint and a sandwich in the Blue Boar he walked to St Thomas's lodge. Zuylestein was fidgeting. He seemed even more on edge than when they had last met and made two or three attempts to extract information. Nat refused to be drawn, explaining that any details he revealed at the current stage of his investigation might well be misleading.

A short corridor from the lodge led directly to St Thomas's fifteenth-century hall, with its polychromed woodwork and portraits of early masters. They crossed the dais behind high table and passed through another door into a passageway beyond. Two flights of stairs brought them to an arched doorway.

Zuylestein opened it and quickly looked inside. 'All clear,' he muttered conspiratorially.

The panelled room they entered was, as Jenny had said, very attractive. It was long but well-proportioned. It was as wide as the building and had windows set into the wall on each side. To the left there were three, each with its own window seat. The wall facing them had one matching window set between the two large, stone fireplaces. The remaining wall space on the right was occupied by closed-in cupboards.

The one that interested Nat was the nearest and he now turned to it.

'What's kept in here?' he asked.

'I haven't the remotest idea,' Zuylestein said.

'May I?' Nat put his hand to the brass handle. He turned it but it did not yield. 'Locked,' he said. 'Do you have a key, Sir Joseph?'

'No, I'm afraid not. Why on earth is it important? I'm sure there's nothing of value or interest in there.'

'Possibly. Possibly not.' Nat fiddled with the handle but the lock held firm. 'What a nuisance. I'm afraid, Sir Joseph, I've wasted your time.'

At that moment the door behind them opened to admit a small, slightly built man with jet-black hair and moustache and eyebrows to match.

'Oh, good afternoon, Master. Happy New Year.' The newcomer's smile bore little suggestion of sincerity.

'Hello, Simeon.' Sir Joseph retained his composure. 'I thought you were in Ireland.'

'We flew back this morning. In-laws are best taken in small doses.' He cast a quizzical glance in Nat's direction.

'I was just showing Dr Gye around. Have you two met?' Zuylestein made the introductions. 'Nathaniel Gye, Simeon Grimm, our college bursar.'

97

'*The* Nathaniel Gye? What a pleasure.' Grimm offered a firm handshake. 'But then I suppose it was bound to be only a matter of time before Cambridge's most celebrated ghostbuster paid St Thomas's a visit. I assume you know Dr Collard and her little gang of psychic eager beavers.'

'We are acquainted,' Nat replied cautiously.

'Then you are probably aware that the college,' he glanced briefly in the master's direction, 'agreed to their investigation against my advice. I felt sure no good could come of it and, tragically, I was proved right.'

Nat replied calmly. 'As I understand it, Professor Hockridge's death was a result of his own impetuosity and not any misbehaviour on the part of Dr Collard or her colleagues.'

Grimm sniffed. 'Try telling that to his grieving widow.' He turned to Zuylestein. 'I assume, Master, that you have heard from the dean confirming the fifteenth as the date for the memorial service.'

'Yes, he did send me a note.'

'Well, let's just hope that that will be the final episode in this absurd saga. I don't wish to belittle your undoubted professionalism, Dr Gye, but I do find it difficult to understand how serious men of science can give credence to superstitious nonsense about "departed spirits".' Grimm emphasized the last two words to make them sound ridiculous. 'Anything untoward that took place on F staircase was either in the minds of highly strung young people or has some natural explanation.'

Nat grabbed the opportunity to test the bursar's unconscious reactions. He watched the other man carefully as he said, with a disarming smile, 'I'm sure you're right, Dr Grimm. Any abnormal activity in this college must be of human origin.'

Grimm's eyelids flickered as he tried to hold Nat's gaze. 'Hmm! Well, it's a relief to have confirmation of one's opinion from such an eminent authority. Anyway, I must not disturb your tour. I only popped in to pick up yesterday's copy of *The Times*.'

He crossed the room to a side table where all the latest newspapers were neatly laid out.

As he made his way back to the door, Sir Joseph asked, 'By the way, Simeon, what do we keep in these cupboards? I've often wondered.'

Grimm sniffed again. 'Bound copies of *Punch*, *Illustrated London News* and the like. They're a blessed nuisance. We could use the space for more important things. We ought to dump them but they came as part of a major bequest to the college library back in the seventies, so we're duty bound to keep them. The key's on the mantelpiece over there in the unlikely event of anyone wishing to consult them.' With a brisk movement he left the room.

Nat stared at the closed door. 'Well, that's put paid to the secrecy of our little pact.'

'Oh, yes. Simeon is very astute. He will be putting two and two together and coming up with whatever answer suits him.' Zuylestein groaned. 'That means we'll have to work even faster to get to the bottom of things. He may try to bring the F5 business up in front of the Visitor and all the fellows at the Epiphany meeting. That's our sort of annual stick-taking.' He sighed. 'So, have you seen all you need? Do you still want to look in this cupboard?'

'Better just check.'

Nat crossed to the nearer fireplace and found the key. He unlocked the cupboard. What confronted him were the dull red spines of dozens of volumes of old books. There was no sign of a ladder.

Back in his room at Beaufort, Nat poured himself a large brandy. Then another. He sat at his window, thinking hard and, at the same time, trying not to think. Images and snatches of conversation came unbidden to his mind but when he tried to grasp them they dissolved again, like the skeletal oaks at the far end of the fellows' garden, drifting in and out of the winter mist. He stared mournfully at the droplets of water falling from the Lebanon cedar in the middle of the lawn. Where had it all gone wrong? He and Kathryn had different careers but they had always managed to dovetail fairly comfortably. Or so he thought. Perhaps he had been deluding himself. Perhaps the contrast had become too stark between the glamorous world of fashion shoots, celebrity interviews and Atlantic-hopping and the staid life of a university teacher. Kathryn had found someone more to her liking and could not bring herself to come clean about it. Nat cursed himself for not seeing the signs earlier. She had certainly been more distant in recent months. And then there were her absurd innuendoes about him and Jenny Collard. He had dismissed that as a jealous whim but now he realized that it was really transferred guilt. Kathryn was trying to convince herself that it was *he* who was betraying their marriage and not she.

So, he was now the cuckolded husband, that evergreen figure of fun. Nat emptied the last drop of VSOP into his glass and hunched in his chair while an early dusk spread gloom outside. He willed inner darkness to obliterate his own thoughts and drifted into half-sleep.

He was roused some time later by the rippling tone of the telephone.

'Ah good, Nathaniel, there you are. Kathryn thought I might find you in college.'

'Yes, Barny, just catching up on some routine paperwork. What can I do for you?'

'It's about friend Tyrone. He is, as I suspected, far too shrewd to be deceived by our little charade. He has spoken with the Suttons and learned of your involvement and it didn't take him long to make the relevant connections. He telephoned a short while ago demanding to know, as he put it, what we thought we were up to.'

'Awkward.'

'Strangely no, dear boy. He huffed and puffed a bit. Protested about us upsetting his clients. Intimated that he knew we'd been put up to it by those "scoundrels" at St Thomas's. But underneath all the bluster I detect a worried man. I called his bluff. Told him he could think what he liked but we would continue our enquiries into the events at St Thomas's, including, if relevant, his involvement therein. That punctured the balloon. He asked could we have a meeting – "lay all our cards on the table" was his chosen cliché – and I suggested lunch tomorrow at the University Arms. I thought it a suitably anonymous venue where our appearance on a quiet January day was unlikely to be observed by anyone connected with the business in question. Would that suit you, Nathaniel?'

'Yes, that'll be fine. Perhaps, at long last, we'll begin to get a few answers to our growing catalogue of questions.'

'Good. I'll make all the arrangements, then. Make sure we have a corner table – not that a reservation is likely to be necessary at this time of year. Shall we say twelve forty-five in the bar?'

Nat put down the receiver then busied himself switching on lights and drawing the curtains. In the bathroom he looked at himself in the mirror. 'Ugh, what a sight,' he muttered. The face that returned his gaze through wire-framed spectacles was pallid and bore more lines than were appropriate for man in his mid-forties. 'You tired, sad old man,' Nat told the face. 'It's no wonder you've lost her.' He decided to freshen up with a quick shower but first he tried to call Jenny. He listened to her answerphone message and then asked her to get back to him asap about the proposed meeting with Andy Rowsell. He added that she could reach him in college or on his mobile but not at home.

He was towelling himself down minutes later when the phone rang. Draping the bathsheet around him, Nat teetered into the living room and picked up the receiver.

'Hello, is that you, Jenny?'

There was a brief silence. Then, icily, 'No, Darling, sorry to disappoint you. It's me. I was just wondering what time you were likely to be back.'

'I'm leaving here in a few minutes. I'll be there in about half an hour.'

'Good. We'll see you then.' The line went dead.

Nat slammed the receiver down. 'Damn, damn, damn, damn, damn!' he shouted.

He dressed and was just leaving when the phone rang again. His response this time was a cautious, 'Hello.'

'Hi, Nat. Jenny here. You called.'

'Yes, I wondered whether you'd made contact with Andy Rowsell.'

'Yes. I spoke with him this morning. He wasn't over the moon at the prospect of talking with us but he did say we could drop in tomorrow afternoon.'

'Good. Whereabouts?'

'He has a flat in Kingston Street. It's off Mill Road, just before you get to the railway.'

'OK, I'll pick you up about four. Look, things are hotting up. We've got to move faster. I'll explain tomorrow. Do you think you could set up an urgent meeting with Dr Cowley? We must get as complete a picture as possible of just what was happening here ten years ago.'

'I'll see what I can do, Nat. See you tomorrow.'

That evening it seemed that the boys were more reluctant than usual to go to bed, although it might have been their parents who were in no hurry to be left alone together. The children provided them with a neutral zone in which they played card games and chatted and laughed at weak jokes. It was almost ten o'clock before goodnights had been said, lights turned out and doors closed. In the living room Nat poured drinks. He and Kathryn sat in deep armchairs, neither of them relaxed. Eventually, it was Kathryn who opened the bowling.

'Good party last night?'

'Not really. I'm getting too old for discos. Not that they ever appealed to me much. How did you know I was at a party?'

'Called about eleven thirty. I didn't like to think of you

102

sitting here, seeing the New Year in with a solitary glass. Where was the party?'

'King's. Friends of Jenny's were throwing it and she asked if I'd like to go. I wasn't going to but when I couldn't reach you by phone, I thought, What the heck?'

'You tried to phone me?'

'Yes. I called the office but some security bloke said you weren't there and hadn't been there all day.'

'Checking up on me, were you?' Kathryn glared across at him.

Nat crashed his empty tumbler down on the table beside him with almost enough force to break it. 'Hey, just a minute!' He tried unsuccessfully to maintain his calm. 'If you call me, it's a display of concern. I call you and I'm accused of checking up on you!'

Kathryn shrugged. 'Forget it,' she said.

'That's a bit difficult. You told me you were spending the whole day in the office but you weren't.'

'So you *are* checking up on me!' Kathryn shouted shrilly.

'If you weren't being so bloody secretive the issue wouldn't arise. Where *were* you yesterday?'

Kathryn jumped up. 'I'm not going to submit to this third-degree treatment.' She strode to the stairs. 'If you don't trust me . . .' The sentence remained unfinished as she mounted the stairs. Seconds later Nat heard the bedroom door slam.

The Eighth Day of Christmas

Nat arrived early in the bar at the University Arms, hoping to get a good look at Paul Tyrone before he was spotted himself. However, as he entered the almost deserted bar, he saw that Barny and their guest were already present.

'Good afternoon, sir.' A bored barman greeted him from the other side of the counter and the two customers standing a few metres away automatically turned in Nat's direction. He only had seconds to form a hasty assessment of Peter Tyrone but his first impression concurred with Barny's. The pinstriped suit was a trifle over-stylish. The plain purple shirt and tie were striving to make a statement.

Barny did the introductions and after a few minutes of small talk, the three men took their drinks into the dining room. They sat at a window table overlooking Parker's Piece, the large open grassed area across which cyclists and pedestrians, well wrapped against the biting easterly wind, made their way, carefully skirting roped-off cricket squares. As soon as they had disposed of menus and the wine list Nat took the initiative.

'Mr Tyrone, you are quite correct in assuming that, in this business of St Thomas's, we have the interests of the college at heart. However, you would be quite wrong to make the further assumption that what we have in mind is a white-wash. On the contrary, we are interested in getting at the facts. Paul Sutton's death was tragic but it was a long time ago. Can you tell us why you want to bring it up again,

105

particularly when it's so painful for the dead man's parents?'

'*I* bring it up?' The lawyer looked genuinely surprised. 'It isn't me who wants the case reopened. I understand you've met the Suttons, Dr Gye, so you'll know that they are obsessed – Mrs Sutton especially – with their son's death. It's been ten years but they still can't put it behind them and move on.'

Barny peered over his spectacles. 'Are you telling us that it was the Suttons who approached you and not vice versa?'

'Absolutely. Look, what happened was this. I had some dealings with them over a probate issue. My firm handled the estate of Mrs Sutton's late father. In the course of conversation it came out that I had actually been at St Tom's at the same time as Paul. They'd never accepted the coroner's verdict of misadventure and they'd convinced themselves that the college was covering something up. Then there was all that "ghost" business. Dr Gye, you won't need me to tell you that people do strange things at the supposed promptings of their departed loved ones. The Suttons begged me to pursue the matter.'

Barny pursed his lips. 'So you became what I believe our American cousins call a "hearse chaser"?'

'That's unfair, Mr Cox. I was doing what I could to help my clients.'

'No doubt for substantial remuneration.'

Tyrone flushed angrily. 'You reckon all law firms should be registered charities?'

Barny opened his mouth to continue the combat but Nat quickly interposed. 'We do seem to have conflicting interpretations of your relationship with the college, Mr Tyrone. From St Thomas's perspective you appear – not to put too fine a point upon it – to be blackmailing them.' The lawyer avoided eye contact and fixedly concentrated on his food. 'Presumably, you believe you have some hold over the college; you know some secret they will pay good money to keep secret.'

When Tyrone made no reply, Nat continued. 'If this is the case – and I'm sure you'll enlighten me if I'm wrong – it does seem to me that you're taking an enormous risk. For an honest man of law to have information about a crime and to seek to profit from that information instead of taking it to the police . . . well . . .'

'The Law Society would be most unhappy,' Barny added.

Tyrone glared across the table. 'Now who's blackmailing who?'

Nat said, 'Look, Mr Tyrone, until and unless the pertinent facts come into the open, suspicion will be rampant and that's no good for the college, it's no good for the Suttons and it's certainly no good for you.'

Tyrone breathed a long sigh and pushed his half-empty plate away. 'OK, so I was bluffing – but with the best of motives.' He paused, as though assembling his thoughts. Nat guessed he was deciding what to say and what not to say. Eventually the lawyer leaned forward and spoke quietly, even though the few other occupants of the dining room were several tables away. 'Look, this all goes back to student days – wild days, irresponsible days. I'm sure you can remember your own. I was in the same year as Paul Sutton so, of course, I knew him – not well but it was impossible not to be very aware of him. He was the star of our intake – brilliant, fun, outrageous, the sun of his own little galaxy. Others clustered around him like dependent planets.'

'And that didn't include you?' Barny enquired.

'No, I didn't belong to the charmed inner circle. The boat club kept me very busy. But I guess I was as shocked as everyone else by Paul's sudden death and the revelations that came out afterwards.'

'You mean the revelations about Sutton being into drugs?' Nat asked. 'Did that come as a complete surprise to you?'

'I think everyone knew or suspected something. Inevitably, there were rumours about just who was involved in

107

Paul's ring. But it was only when the police invaded the college and interviewed us all that the scale of his operation began to emerge. Friends one had never suspected turned out to be users. The governing body was stunned.'

'I can imagine,' Nat said. 'What repercussions were there?'

'Very few eventually. The fellows were desperate to keep the lid on as tight as possible. We were tacitly warned that speaking to the press would be a rustication matter.'

'Was anyone sent down?' Barny asked.

'No. Three members of the undergraduate body were charged with possession but they all received short suspended sentences and the college decided not to take disciplinary action.'

Nat looked surprised. 'Didn't that strike you as unduly lenient, given the current alarm at the spread of narcotics trading in Cambridge and the authorities' determination to clamp down on it?'

'I suppose so – but, then, we were all on the side of the culprits and against what we saw as "oppressive" authority. Some people even suggested . . .' Tyrone stopped abruptly.

'Yes?' Nat prompted.

'Nothing. Ten-year-old student gossip isn't worth repeating. Anyway, all this blew up in my last term when I had other things to worry about. I was determined not to let the stupidity of other people ruin my degree chances.'

'Which, manifestly, it didn't,' Barny observed. 'You've done well for yourself.'

'Let's say I've been lucky.'

'A partnership, at your age?' That suggests more than good luck.'

Tyrone shrugged. 'I was working for a law firm in Aldeburgh, mainly so that I could indulge my passion for sailing, when I met Sally. I didn't know that her father was a solicitor in Watford who was on the lookout for a promising junior. We married. I joined the family business – and the rest, as they say, is . . .'

'Nepotism?' Barny suggested.

Tyrone scowled. 'I'm a good lawyer! I earn my keep!'

'This is getting us away from the point,' Nat said. 'When did you meet the Suttons?'

'A couple of years ago. As I said, I helped to wind up Jane's father's estate. Of course, it was some time before I put two and two together. Sutton's a common enough name.'

'And when they realized the connection, they persuaded you to look into their son's death?'

'Jane is a very persuasive woman. She claimed that Paul had come through to her in séances and told her to find out the truth – just as, later, she made the same appeal to you. She's a desperate woman, clutching at whatever straws she can find. I felt sorry for her – for them both. Their life is a living hell. Jane inherited her father's house and after we'd sold it she was pretty well off. I suggested that they ought to move, perhaps abroad, and make a new life for themselves. But Jane was insistent that, whatever it cost, she would clear her son's name.'

'What did she think you could do?'

'Heaven knows, Dr Gye! She convinced herself that our meeting was "destiny", that somehow Paul had engineered it from beyond the grave.'

'So what, in fact, *did* you do?' Barny asked.

'I got hold of all the press reports covering Paul's death and the subsequent investigation.'

'And discovered?'

'Nothing.' Tyrone gave a frustrated shake of the head. 'There was nothing to discover. The coroner, the police, the reporters – all were in agreement. Paul Sutton died of a self-inflicted overdose of heroin.'

'So why the threats to St Thomas's? Why the bluff?'

At that moment the waiter appeared to clear the table and take orders for coffee. Nat was annoyed. The pause gave Tyrone time to compose his reply.

At length the lawyer said, 'It was the only other thing I could think of to do. *If* there was some secret lurking in the college which only one or more of the senior members knew, I thought I might be able to panic them into revealing it. If I could give the Suttons something – anything – it might have helped them to obtain closure.'

Nat asked, 'What was your reaction to Professor Hockridge's death?'

For the first time Tyrone smiled. 'It was odd. Fitting, perhaps.'

'Would you care to explain?'

'Well, Paul and Hockridge were very close in life and now, it seems, they are close in death. The professor – only, of course, he wasn't a professor then – was Paul's supervisor. But he was much more. Despite the difference in their ages, they were remarkably good friends.'

After lunch Nat and Barny made their way back to Beaufort deep in conversation.

'Did you believe him?' Nat asked.

'I think Mr Tyrone's story is what my grandmother would have called a poor man's stew – lots of gravy and very little meat.'

'Yes, it was very carefully calculated, wasn't it? He told us just enough to disarm us, and not a scrap more.'

'Still, you must be happy that you've fulfilled your contract with Sir Joseph Zuylestein. Friend Tyrone has been well and truly scared off and his bluff called. St Thomas's should have no more trouble from him. You can report back to the master on a job well done.'

'Ye . . . s. I suppose so.'

They crossed the road outside Emmanuel College and set off along Pembroke Street.

'Why the hesitant response?'

Nat pondered his reply. 'I don't know. I suppose it was Tyrone's sudden climbdown. He has St Thomas's over a barrel and ready to buy him off handsomely. Then he suddenly throws in the towel. Says it was all a big bluff and he's ready to retire gracefully. Why?'

'Presumably, to persuade us to follow suit.'

'Exactly. Which means there *is* something to find out.'

'Something he wants to exploit himself, without our competition.'

'Perhaps.' Nat stopped suddenly and a cyclist emerging from the Cavendish Laboratories almost collided with him. 'But supposing it's closer to home than that? Supposing Tyrone has a guilty secret and we're getting too close to it for comfort.'

'That would make sense,' Barny agreed, as they resumed their walk. 'However much he was hoping to squeeze out of the college it wouldn't be enough to compensate him for public disgrace and the loss of his career.'

'I'd love to know how close Tyrone really was to Sutton back in those heady, undergraduate days. He was very concerned to convince us that he was only on the outer rim of the charmed circle.'

'Hmm, I wonder . . .'

'What, Barny?'

'Well, it may have no bearing, but, by his own admission, Peter Tyrone is a keen yachtsman who keeps a boat on the east coast. I wonder if he had his own vessel ten years ago.'

'You mean . . .'

'Drugs. They had to come into the country somehow and Aldeburgh – or wherever – can't be much more than an hour and a half's drive from Cambridge.'

'It's a thought,' Nat admitted. After a pause he said, 'Interesting about the connection between Hockridge and Sutton. What do you suppose Tyrone meant by them being "close"?'

'Zeus and Ganymede, I presume. Middle-aged man and beautiful youth. Not exactly a unique relationship in our introverted, little university world.'

'But still, even in this liberated age, a love that is sometimes reluctant to speak its name.'

'Oh, certainly. For Hockridge to come out of the closet would have done little to enhance his career, let alone his marriage.'

111

Nat mused aloud. 'Secrets. That's what this whole business increasingly seems to revolve around. Paul Sutton, an assiduous collector of secrets.' An image flashed into his mind of Paul Sutton's room.

'Careful, dear boy.' Barny introduced a note of caution. 'We've only been speculating about Hockridge. For all we know . . .'

'Of course. We mustn't jump to conclusions but if Sutton and Hockridge . . .'

They emerged into Trumpington Street opposite Beaufort's impressive gate tower and waited at the kerbside for a break in the traffic.

'Talking about Hockridge,' Nat asked, 'do you know what happened about the funeral?'

'It's at Fen Stavely tomorrow morning. The inquest and then the holiday held things up. I gather it's to be a very quiet, family affair. Apparently the widow is adamant about not having any representation from the college.'

'Hmm! It would be interesting to meet Mrs Hockridge. Unfortunately, I have a faculty meeting.'

A driving-school car emerged judderingly from Silver Street, then came to a sudden halt as the driver stalled the engine. Taking advantage of the gap in the traffic, Nat and Barny strode across the road.

'I get the distinct impression that I'm being deputed to funeral duty,' Barny said as they entered the college.

'It would be interesting to hear what the angry widow knows or suspects about her husband's death . . . but, of course . . .'

'Say no more, Nathaniel. I shall don the dark grey worsted and put in a discreet appearance. At my age funerals are almost routine events.'

Nat spent an hour going through the papers for the following day's meeting, then collected his car and went to pick up Jenny. On their way to Andy Rowsell's home he reported on the latest developments.

112

'Ah, well, there you are, then!' Jenny's eyes gleamed enthusiastically.

'Oh, exactly where am I?' Nat braked for the red light at a pedestrian crossing and glared at a group of boys who had pressed the button just for the pleasure of bringing traffic to a standstill. 'What do you mean?' The lights changed and he continued along Fen Causeway.

'Well, all that business of a secret way into F5. It was an ingenious idea, Nat, and I'm sure I saw a ladder. Now it's mysteriously disappeared. So, I think we must be back with a supernatural explanation.'

Nat nodded. 'I should have checked that sighting myself.'

'You think I imagined it.'

'I think it may have been a trick of the light.'

'What about a Fortean phenomenon – something appearing where it shouldn't be. If someone *did* put a ladder in that cupboard years ago to get into the attic it could re-manifest itself, as Charles Fort claimed back in the 1920s.'

'It could also be auto-suggestion. We were looking for a ladder and we – you – saw one.'

Jenny was not to be deterred. 'Whatever the explanation, you can't deny there's some powerful force at work here and I think what we now know about Paul and old Hockridge is very suggestive. They had an intense relationship. Were probably up to their ears together in something very seamy. What if they fell out – a lovers' tiff, quarrel over drug profits or whatever. And what if Paul ended up dead? Just think of all that psychic energy locked up in F5.'

'It's a theory.'

'You don't buy it?'

'To test it we'd have to eliminate beyond a shadow of doubt the possibility of human agency. Even then, sceptics would put the spasmodic hauntings down to hallucination or conditioning – people seeing or hearing what they expect to see or hear.'

'But at least we've proved that no flesh and blood person can get into that room now except by the staircase.'

113

'We didn't explore the loft thoroughly. I think it's very likely that there is another way up. Probably a hatch over one of the stairwells. That's fairly conventional in these old buildings. Anyway, if you think about it you'll realize that there doesn't have to be a hidden way into F5.'

'But that's ridic—'

'No. There is one member of the governing body who can come and go anywhere in the college without attracting attention. You, yourself, said he'd be your prime suspect.'

'You mean Grimm?'

Nat negotiated the turn into Mill Road. 'The bursar has access to all the keys. He may even have his own set. And I agree with your estimate of him. He is a rather objectionable little man.'

'Ah, but,' Jenny said with a note of triumph, 'there was absolutely no one else in that room or on the staircase the night the professor died.'

'I grant you that, which means we're back to square one on that particular event.'

'No, no!' Jenny pummelled the dashboard excitedly. 'We've been looking at everything the wrong way round. It's not a question of something threatening or attacking Hockridge. What we have is a psychic projection *by* Hockridge. Just think of all the emotion building up in him over the years. How awful it must feel to carry the guilt and anguish of having deliberately murdered someone you love. So, Hockridge walks up that dark staircase towards the very place where he killed Paul. And he goes into a kind of emotional overload. You've read Rossheim's paper on the Hamburg manifestations. This fits his theory perfectly. Hockridge *saw* his victim on the staircase because his own unconscious projected an image. That would explain why nothing was picked up on camera.'

'Well, hopefully we can check that now. This is Kingston Street.' Nat swung the car to the left.

'Andy's is over there – the house with the green paint.'

114

Jenny indicated one of a row of semis that had been converted into flats. 'He's on the first floor.'

Minutes later the door was opened to them by a blonde young woman in nurse's uniform. Jenny introduced her briefly as Vicky and Nat noticed the tired eyes that a welcoming smile could not hide.

In the narrow hallway Vicky said, 'He's in the kitchen on baby duty. I'm just off to work. For heaven's sake go quietly. I've just got Debs off to sleep. It's the devil of a job at the moment. She's teething.' She led the way up the stairs. At the top she moved a folding pushchair which was partly blocking the small landing. 'Leave your coats here, if you can find somewhere.' Vicky indicated a row of pegs hung with clothes, umbrellas and fishing tackle. Nat found a place for his overcoat on top of a black travelling bag, a retractable dog lead and a supermarket carrier which seemed to be full of string.

Vicky pushed open a door. 'I'm off,' she announced. 'If Debs wakes, her bottle is beside the cot.' She squeezed past the visitors and was gone.

Andy Rowsell was hunched over the kitchen table working at something which involved wire, coloured cotton and tiny feathers. He looked up and gave the most cursory of nods.

'I see you make your own flies,' Nat said as an opening gambit.

'Commercial ones are too bloody expensive,' Andy muttered.

Unbidden, Nat and Jenny seated themselves at the table opposite their reluctant host.

Jenny said, 'Come on, Andy, don't be a grouch. We won't bother you for long. Dr Gye just wants to go over the St Tom's business.'

'Why?' Andy frowned with concentration as he wound wire round the shaft of a vicious-looking fishhook.

'I just wondered whether you'd remembered any little details which haven't come out before.'

'I mean, why bother? The old fool died of a heart attack. End of story.'

Nat tried a different tack. 'Did you know Professor Hockridge well?'

Andy shrugged. 'Went to a couple of lectures – pretty crappy.'

Jenny said, 'I thought you reckoned he was quite good in seminars.'

'He had some interesting ideas,' Andy conceded, 'but he was still stuck in the old world of particle physics. We've moved way beyond that.'

'I was wondering if we could have a look at the film you took,' Nat said.

Andy shook his head firmly. 'Number one: all my gear's in a lock-up a couple of streets away and I can't leave here because of the baby. Number two, I've wiped the tapes. Number three, there was nothing on them anyway.'

'That must have been very disappointing. It would have been a real coup to capture on film whatever it was that frightened Professor Hockridge.'

'I'm more interested in detecting and measuring energy fields.'

'And did your equipment detect any anomalies at St Thomas's?'

'Nope.'

Jenny and Nat exchanged gestures of frustration and a long silence followed. It was broken by the sound of a baby crying.

'Bugger it!' Andy threw down the pliers he was using and jumped to his feet. 'Can't get any peace in this fucking place!' He marched from the room.

Without a word the visitors stood up and followed him out. While Nat was collecting his overcoat and gingerly extracting a length of fishing line that had become entangled with it, Jenny called out, 'Thanks a lot, Andy. We'll be off now.'

Back in the car, Jenny said, 'Sorry, Nat, that was a complete waste of time.'

Nat shrugged. 'What a very angry young man.'

'Yes.' Jenny paused. 'He's rude and self-obsessed and, yet, in a way I feel sorry for him. By all accounts he's a brilliant scientist but his personality keeps getting in the way of his advancement.'

'How so?'

'He's having problems completing his PhD thesis. According to him he's so far in advance of the examiners that they can't appreciate his ideas.'

'Presumably, because they insist on him providing adequate experimental proof for those ideas.'

'I guess so.'

'Not an uncommon problem We have to maintain the integrity of the qualification but that sometimes means making really bright students jump through hoops that don't really help them.'

'Anyway, we're not getting anywhere with the professor's death, are we? I guess it'll have to remain an enigma.'

Much of the return journey through rush hour traffic passed in gloomy silence. They avoided the one-way system and they were skirting Midsummer Common before Jenny said what was on her mind.

'So, are we calling it a day now that you've got Tyrone out of the way?'

'It will certainly be a relief to get back to some sort of normality.' Even as Nat said it he realized that life at home was anything but normal. He and Kathryn would have to have the conversation they had both been avoiding.

'Only I must tell Sandra Cowley that we're not going to meet her. Pity, she sounded really keen to talk about the Sutton gang.'

'I didn't know you'd managed to set up another meet.'

'I haven't had a chance to mention it till now. She's actually coming to Newmarket tomorrow for an NHS conference. I tentatively fixed to see her about six o'clock, but we mustn't waste her time if we're dropping the case.'

'No, that wouldn't be fair. Better call her and cancel.'

'OK.'

Silence returned and a couple of minutes later Nat pulled up outside the house Jenny shared with a couple of friends. She got out and stood by the front door fumbling for her key. She had just found it and inserted it in the lock when Nat lowered his side window and called out.

'Jenny.'

'Yes?' She turned.

'On second thoughts, let's leave the arrangement with Dr Cowley.'

The Ninth Day of Christmas

Fen Stavely had three shocks in store for Barny Cox. The first was the clarity of his memory about the place. The second was the extent to which the village had changed. The third came later in the day. The village was no more than a dozen miles from Cambridge but the old lawyer realized that more than forty years had passed since his last visit. The image of that day was vivid – the spring sunshine, the smell of new-mown grass, the two bicycles propped against the lych gate and the bench where he and Caroline had sat to share their sandwiches. He could even conjure up the taste of liver pâté and tomatoes – why was it that tomatoes were sweeter and more tender in the 1950s than the thick-skinned monstrosities of today's supermarkets? But that was not all that had altered out of recognition. In those far-off days when he had practised law instead of teaching it, Fen Stavely had been no more than a cluster of houses round a green. Now, access to its ancient heart was cluttered with residential developments. Then there had been little to disturb the rural calm. Now bird song had to compete with the thrumming of traffic on the M11, not half a mile away. On that distant day when he and Caroline had become engaged St Mark's church had stood, slightly aloof, amidst fields on the edge of the village. Now it was surrounded on three sides by the characterless monotony of 'desirable residences'. It was with a sense almost of personal affront that Barny locked the car door and directed his steps towards the church. Places should not be allowed to regress in this haphazard way.

119

He wished he had not come. A grey sky threatened more rain and the dripping yews bordering the path to the Norman south door were doing their utmost to appear unwelcoming. The church was sure to be cold and the brief office for the burial of the dead could offer little in the way of comfort to a seasoned agnostic, conscious that he was not far from the brink of that unknown over which Jeremy Hockridge had already plunged. He paused to gaze across the acre of leaning and sagging gravestones.

> Golden lads and girls all must,
> As chimney sweepers, come to dust.

That included his own golden girl.

Barny shook his head to dispel memory and entered the church. It *was* cold – and damp. He seated himself in a back pew and gazed around the interior. If memory served, St Mark's, all those years ago, had been devoid of clutter. Now there was an array of altar furniture and, here and there, gaudy statues of saints and a particularly hideous one of the virgin with a votive lamp burning before it. Fen Stavely church had obviously moved up (or down?) the ecclesiological ladder in the Catholic direction. Barny wondered if the mourners were in for a high church service, strong on ritual and weak on spiritual content. Any doubt was removed minutes later when the door reopened and a rotund, fiftyish clergyman entered. Barny noted the well-made suit – just the right shade of dark grey – the florid features and the cursory nod in the direction of the altar as the vicar strode with well-practised, purposeful strides into his vestry. 'Jobbing cleric,' Barny muttered under his breath and returned to his own thoughts.

Why had he agreed to attend the funeral of a man he had scarcely ever met during all the years they had both served the same university? Was it just a desire to help young Gye? He was grateful enough to Nathaniel, a sensitive fellow who understood something of the boredom and loneliness of a retired academic who longed for mental stimulus. So, if Nathaniel thought his presence at those obsequies could achieve anything, Barny would certainly do his best, though, for the life of him, he could not imagine that he would learn anything on this dark and dismal morning. No, there was more to it than that. The magic of a name – Fen Stavely. That compelling melancholy of returning to a place which held such poignant memories. What was that Dante tag implanted in a long-past classical education? 'Nothing is sadder than recalling happy days during times of misfortune.'

The door opened again and the first members of the congregation entered. The vicar bustled up the aisle to meet them, now cassocked and sporting a long cloak with an unnecessarily showy crimson lining. Minutes later the coffin arrived, followed by a small family group of mourners. Barny had his first glimpse of Mrs Hockridge. What was immediately apparent was that here was no suffering widow. If she was heavily burdened by grief she was stoically containing her emotion. She was a tall, muscular woman who carried herself with great dignity and for this solemn occasion she had chosen to wear a russet topcoat and no hat. Her immaculately coiffed steel-grey hair framed a very square face and her blue eyes stared straight before her. '*Femme formidable*' was the phrase that sprang inevitably to Barny's mind.

From his vantage point near the tower arch he followed the service, an observer rather than a participant, a fact for which he felt a twinge of guilt. He was relieved when the first part of the ritual was over and the vicar advanced down the aisle leading the funeral director's men with the coffin. Once again Barny had a good look at the professor's widow as she came towards him. At the crossing she paused and looked straight at him with a quizzically raised eyebrow. Barny found her brief attention slightly unnerving but the glance lasted a mere fraction of a second before she turned to the left to follow the coffin out of the building.

Barny was the last to leave the church. Outside, the air was moist with something between mist and rain and he raised his umbrella before following the little procession towards the far corner of the churchyard. He watched the interment at a distance and was minded to slip away as soon as he decently could. He was forestalled by Mrs Hockridge. She shook hands briefly with the vicar then walked briskly from the graveside and stationed herself beside the lych gate, the perfect hostess doing her duty by her guests. As he approached her at the end of the queue, Barny prepared a few formal words of condolence but he never got to utter them.

'You are Barnaby Cox,' the widow said, extending a gloved hand. It seemed almost an accusation.

'Yes,' he confessed, striving to recover his poise. 'I'm sorry, I didn't realize we had met.'

The thin lips formed themselves into a faint smile. '*Tempora mutantur, et nos mutamur in illis*. Join us at the George. Nothing elaborate.' She turned and walked briskly towards a car where the undertaker was holding a door open for her.

Barny racked his brain as he went in search of his own vehicle. Where had they met before? The Latin tag suggested that they had known each other many years ago. He dimly recognized the line but could not locate its origin. 'Times change and we change with them.'

The George, despite its name, was a brick-built Victorian building of unprepossessing appearance but the small parlour into which he was shown was comfortably furnished and a welcome fire blazed in the hearth. Barny accepted a glass of dry sherry and gratefully warmed himself while watching Mrs Hockridge do her duty round of the dozen or so guests. At last she approached him.

'Well, Barny, have you worked it out yet, or has time been more cruel to me than to you?'

He shook his head ruefully. 'I'm afraid you still have the advantage of me, Mrs Hockridge.'

122

She laughed. 'Forget the "Mrs Hockridge". Try Madge Hennessy.'

Barny gasped. 'Good Lord! Can it really be . . .?'

'It not only can; it is.'

'Gracious me! After all these years . . . I'm lost for words.'

Again there came a soft, low laugh. 'As I recall, that's a rare state of affairs. Now, look,' she went on brusquely, 'you shan't escape again. Grab yourself a sandwich or two while I wind things up here. As soon as I've got rid of these tiresome people you can walk me home. We have several decades of catching up to do.'

It was more than an hour later that Barny was seated in what was the extremely well-appointed eighteenth-century drawing room of Stavely Lodge, a substantial house in its own grounds, which had succeeded in warding off the brick and tile sprawl of new development and still looked out over wide, flat fenland fields. By then he had filled in the basic details of the missing years. Back in the 1950s Madge had been part of the crowd of young graduates to which he and Caroline had also belonged. The gang had inevitably split up as its members went their several ways, promising faithfully to keep in touch. Eventually, only Caroline had been left finishing off her PhD studies and Barny, in practice in London, came back as often as possible to be with her. By then Madge Hennessy had secured a post at St Andrews University, where, as she explained, she met and married Jeremy Hockridge.

She entered the room with a tray of tea things which she set on a low table between them. 'It was several months before I heard about Caroline,' she said. 'I should have written but, by then, it seemed too late. I was, of course, desperately sorry. Did you eventually find someone else?'

'No. After a couple of years I resumed my academic career – clambered into the university box and shut the lid. By the time I got round to peeping out again all I could see was a very different world. Frenzied – or perhaps just younger.'

Madge poured tea into fine porcelain cups. 'To think that for all these years you've been just a few miles away and we've never met.'

'When did you come back?'

'Jeremy obtained his fellowship at St Thomas's twelve years ago and he got his chair four years later. I wasn't keen on returning to Cambridge. I made it a condition of coming with him that we bought a house in Fen Stavely. Such happy memories. Nostalgia. Trying to conjure up the ghosts of the past. Stupid.'

'I get the impression – and forgive me if I'm speaking out of turn – that, you and Jeremy . . .'

'That ours was not a marriage created in heaven? We, neither of us, made a secret of it. Jeremy was . . . well, bisexual would, I think, be a euphemism. He chose not to tell me till after we were married. That was typical of the man. He lived life entirely on his own terms. He was devious, cantankerous and selfish. I think I was probably the only person he couldn't bully.'

'Why did you stay together?'

'I suppose, like you, I was disinclined to look outside the box. It was a very comfortable box. At the cost of acting the charming hostess at college and faculty functions and being nice to Jeremy's students I got to enjoy a very agreeable lifestyle and indulge my own interests. As regards sex – in those years when it seemed important – well, let's just say I didn't miss out.'

'Even so, Jeremy's death – or the circumstances sur-rounding it – must have come as something of a shock.'

'Bizarre, wasn't it?'

'You haven't formed any theory about it?'

Madge shook her head. 'I demanded an explanation from the college. I thought that would be expected of me. I also made it quite clear I didn't want St Thomas's involved in the funeral. Of course, Jeremy would have loved to be buried with full honours but that would have been the ultimate hypocrisy.'

124

'Why so?'

'Because he hated the lot of them. Master, fellows, the whole shooting match. He held them in utter contempt. He liked the students – or most of them – but he couldn't stand his contemporaries.'

'Did he ever mention a student of his by the name of Paul Sutton?'

Madge raised her eyebrows in surprise. 'Paul Sutton? Oh yes, but why the interest? Oh, that ghost nonsense, I suppose.' She sat back in the armchair and closed her eyes. 'Paul Sutton. Yes, Jeremy had quite a thing going with him. But, then, my husband was not the world's best judge of character.'

'You didn't like Sutton?'

'Let's just say that the two of them deserved each other. Now, another cup?'

As Barny watched his hostess wield teapot and milk jug he wondered how far he dared press his enquiries. Having resurrected a very old friendship the last thing he wanted to do was spoil everything with intrusive questions. He decided on a change of subject. 'Will you go on living in this house?'

But Madge Hockridge countered his strategy. She stared at him with remarkably clear and intelligent blue eyes. 'Now, Barny Cox, suppose you tell me why you are really here.'

Barny smiled. 'Dear Madge, I never could outsmart you, could I?'

'No, and I certainly haven't lost my marbles yet. So?'

Barny gave her a potted version of the St Thomas's problem while Madge pursed her lips and listened in silence. 'So,' he concluded, 'we're just trying to get as clear a picture as possible of what was going on in the college all those years ago.' He watched anxiously for Madge's reaction. Once again she surprised him.

She threw back her head in a deep-throated laugh. 'How deliciously exciting! I do love a good scandal!' Then she added, suddenly serious, 'I wonder if Sir Joseph realizes just what he is stirring up. It might be wiser to let sleeping dogs lie.'

'Unfortunately, these dogs are very much awake – and barking noisily.'

'Yes, I see that . . . And yet . . .' For some moments she stared out of the window. 'We have to assess, do we not, what is the *summum bonum*, the highest good.'

'Are you suggesting that there are some things which should remain swept under the carpet?'

'The period you are talking about was a very unhappy one in the life of St Tom's. Of course, we mere wives never officially knew everything that was going on but . . . well . . . I like to think I was intelligent enough to fill in most of the gaps correctly.'

Barny leaned forward eagerly. 'And?'

Madge shook her head. 'No, no, you are not to press me. I have to give this careful thought. You see, the bad times passed. The necessary action was taken – some of it drastic. The college settled down to doing what it's supposed to do. If you turn the spotlight back on those years there are certain people . . .' She stopped abruptly and sank back against the cushions.

Barny was suddenly concerned. 'Madge, I'm sorry. This is very thoughtless of me. I shouldn't be outstaying my welcome, today of all days.'

'Nonsense! Seeing you again is the best thing that's happened to me for a long time. We must meet again soon. But I am feeling a bit tired. Obviously today has taken more of a toll than I anticipated.'

Barny rose and Madge escorted him to the front door. There she clasped his hand warmly and held it for several seconds. 'I have to sort through all Jeremy's papers. If I come across anything pertinent I'll let you know.'

'Please don't go to any trouble. I feel guilty about bothering you at all. Anyway, Sir Joseph has given us a deadline. Our investigations, successful or otherwise, have to cease before the Epiphany Feast and that's in three days' time.'

126

Madge smiled. 'Ah yes, the Epiphany Feast. Do you know, they've invited me this year. Guilty conscience, I suppose.' Her face brightened suddenly. 'I've just had a brilliant thought. I have no escort. Will you do me the honour?'

'I should be delighted but isn't it rather short notice?'

'Nonsense. I'll phone the steward and tell him I need a masculine arm to lean on. He's fool enough to believe me. So that's settled.'

'I shall look forward to it. Goodbye, Madge.' He turned to leave.

Before he had gone a couple of paces Madge called out, 'One more thing. I don't know how religious you are, Barny, but would you not agree with me that a crime is not necessarily a sin?'

This day, 3 January, saw the welcome return to the Gye household of Suzanne, their au pair. It meant that Nat and Kathryn could get back to their normal working routines. Kathryn usually spent three days a week in her London office and Nat was able to be in college when necessary without having to negotiate with his wife over who should be at home with the children. It also provided the opportunity for the two of them to spend some time together. The mounting tension between them had been intensified by the need to conceal it from the boys.

'How about we go out for lunch?' Nat suggested. Breakfast was over. Ed and Jerry were upstairs showing Suzanne their Christmas presents. Kathryn was sitting on the sofa with her feet curled beneath her, sorting the mail.

'I suppose we could,' she replied distractedly. 'Are we celebrating something?'

'I think we both know we need to talk.'

'Really?' Kathryn appeared absorbed in a long letter with an American stamp on the envelope. 'OK, if you say so.'

'What do you mean, "If I say so"?' Nat struggled to remain calm. 'Something's not right between us and I want to know why. If we don't face up to it we can't do anything about it.'

Kathryn laid the letter aside and looked up. 'Yes, it would be good to get out for lunch. As it happens, I *do* have something to tell you but I'm not ready yet.'

'What the hell . . .!'

The phone rang. Nat grabbed up the receiver. 'Hello!' he almost shouted.

'Nat, is that you?' He recognized the voice of Kathryn's father.

'Ted, hello. Good to hear you. How was your flight back?'

'Oh . . . er . . . yes . . . fine, just fine. How are you all?'

Nat made small talk for a couple of minutes then handed the phone to Kathryn. While she talked with her father he went to his study.

He had been working at the computer screen for a quarter of an hour or so when Kathryn put her head round the door. 'Sorry, I'll have to take a rain check on lunch. Got to go up to London.'

'Meeting him, are you?'

Kathryn did a quick doubletake. 'Who, Dad? He's in America.'

'I didn't mean your father . . . Oh, forget it!' He turned back to the screen.

Twenty minutes later he heard Kathryn go out.

Nat's first assessment of Sandra Cowley was that she was a 'sensible-looking' woman. That certainly did not mean unattractive; her welcoming smile was, in itself, heart-warming. It was just that everything about her – clothes, make-up, body language – exuded a serene competence. Nat thought that, as a doctor, she must be very reassuring. When he and Jenny entered the hotel there were little clusters of people with name badges on dotted around. Almost immediately a fair-haired woman in a cornflower-blue dress detached herself from one of the groups and came across the foyer.

'Hello, Jenny,' she said, with that disarming smile. 'Perfect timing. We've just finished our last plenary of the day.'

Jenny made the introductions.

Nat said, 'May we offer you dinner?'

'That would be great,' Sandra replied, 'as long as we can go somewhere else. I need to escape. You know what they say about doctors; we're like manure; spread out over the ground we can do some good but piled in a heap, we pong!' She removed her name badge. 'I'll just fetch my coat and then I'll be all yours.'

They found a small Italian restaurant in the High Street and ensconced themselves at a corner table as far as possible from the loudspeaker emitting sugary, orchestral versions of Neapolitan songs.

Nat said, 'It's very good of you to give us some of your time.'

'Not at all. I was only too glad to escape for the evening. I've had more than enough shop for one day. Anyway, I'm intrigued and delighted that you're opening up the Sutton business. Since Jenny came to see me I've been giving a lot of thought to it. I even managed to dig out some photographs.' She opened her handbag and took out an envelope. 'Here's Paul Sutton as he wanted the world to see him.' She laid down a coloured print of a rakish young man standing possessively beside a red sports car. An exuberant signature crossed one corner with the legend, 'For Sandra. Thanks for last night.' 'Don't read anything into those words,' she said. 'They were Paul's idea of a joke.'

Jenny wrinkled her nose as she gazed at the picture. 'He obviously thought of himself as on a par with film stars and pop idols.'

'Certainly,' Sandra agreed. 'He scattered these signed photos around like confetti.'

'His old room in his parents' house is full of them.' Nat described the "shrine" where Paul's memory was still revered by a doting mother.

'I feel so sorry for his parents,' Sandra said. 'He treated them abysmally. Never invited them up to Cambridge. They would have tarnished the image he was so carefully creating. I remember them turning up once, unexpectedly. A few of us were having drinks in Paul's room and this perfectly nice couple with a rather apologetic demeanour came in. Paul was furious and he covered it up with cynicism. He went out of his way to humiliate his own mother and father in front of us. It was terribly embarrassing.'

'Yuk.' Jenny turned the photo face down on the table-cloth.

'Yuk, indeed,' Sandra agreed. '"Evil" is a word one hesitates to use of any human being but in Paul Sutton's case it fits the bill. He had that seductive charm one can only call devilish. He flattered women and joshed men. Made us feel we were all part of some privileged brother-hood, the *cognoscenti* of our student era. He formed his own dining club and organized sumptuous meals in St Tom's.' She selected another photograph and slid it across the table. 'Of course, it was all a game to him. He was laughing at us. Using us.'

Nat scrutinized the picture of young men and women in evening dress seated around a long table set with sparkling glass and china. 'Isn't that Peter Tyrone?' He pointed to the person sitting opposite Sutton.

'That's right.' Sandra nodded. 'The other apostle.'

'Apostle?' Jenny queried.

'Yes, you know – Peter and Paul. We always called them the apostles.'

'They were that close?' Nat asked.

'Thick as thieves. That, in itself, is indicative of Sutton's power. You know how undergrads have always tended to divide between hearties and arties. Well, Tyrone was a considerable athlete. He was president of the St Tom's boat club with all the social cachet that went with it. The college first eight had an *annus mirabilis* under his leadership. They were head of the river for the first time in living memory

130

and went on to do well at Henley. Sutton, by contrast, never did a day's exercise in his life. Yet it was Sutton who drew Tyrone into his orbit and appointed him his unofficial deputy.'

'Interesting.' Nat looked thoughtful. 'What did the college authorities make of all this?'

'Amused tolerance, I suppose. That's the standard attitude of fellows to the "young ladies and gentlemen", isn't it?'

Nat smiled. 'Well, I like to think that most of us are a bit more involved than that.'

Sandra laughed. 'Sorry, that wasn't meant to be a blow below the belt. I suppose it's not altogether easy to strike the right balance between respected detachment and friendly support. Actually, I got the impression that one or two of the St Tom's fellows fell over backwards to be too chummy with the student body.'

'Who, for instance?'

'Ah, now we're getting into the realm of gossip and rumour.'

'Oh good,' Jenny said gleefully.

Sandra lifted her glass and sipped appreciatively. 'This wine's nice.'

Nat nodded. 'Yes, it's very enterprising of this place to stock tignanello. Quite a rarity in our country.' He, too, savoured the red liquid.

'Hey, come on, you two!' Jenny protested. 'Can we get back to the point?'

'Paul Sutton fancied himself as a wine buff,' Sandra said. 'He was very thick with Tristram Philigrew who ran a wine society. What was it they called themselves?' She closed her eyes in concentration. 'The Bacchians, that was it. In fact, according to what one of the St Tom's girls told me, Philigrew was the only one of the fellows who was visibly moved by Paul's death. The master called the whole college together in hall and told them what had happened. Apparently Philigrew fainted and had to be helped to a chair.'

131

'The news must have come as a shock to lots of people, especially Sutton's disciples,' Nat suggested.

Sandra frowned. 'Do you know I can't remember any of them being really fazed by it. It all happened very close to exam time. Paul's contemporaries had their heads full of finals and May Balls and going down parties and moving on to face the grey world of work. I suppose for those who were really close to Paul his death marked a dramatic end to their salad days. He had presided over a giddy, glittering, abandoned court and it died with him. The golden era came to an end with a bang instead of a whimper but it was going to come to an end anyway.'

'Look,' Jenny interposed, 'we're getting away from the point again. We were talking about Paul's relationship with senior college members.' Seeing the disapproving looks on the faces of her companions, she added, 'It could be important. We are talking drugs and blackmail here.'

Sandra said, 'I really don't want to blacken reputations, even if all this did happen years ago.'

'I see that,' Nat nodded gravely. 'But Jenny does have a point. You've already told us that Paul Sutton wasn't above extorting money. Maybe he didn't stop at his own contemporaries.'

Sandra shrugged. 'Well, OK, but do remember this is only common room gossip. There was Sandy Sanderson, now the highly respected Professor Sanderson. He was my supervisor in anatomy, so I knew him quite well. He had a penchant for nubile eighteen-year-old freshers.' She sighed. 'Actually, that's more than rumour. He tried it on with me and I know at least one girl who succumbed.'

Nat said, 'He wouldn't be the first or last don to take advantage of his position in that way.'

'True, but there were stories that he gave good exam marks in return for sexual favours.'

'That could certainly have ditched his academic career,' Nat said. 'Were there any stories attaching to Jeremy Hockridge?'

'Hockridge! Well, there were plenty of people who'd have liked to see him discredited.'

'He was unpopular?'

'Yes and no. He could be, by turns, a bully and a benevolent uncle. He had his favourites and, if you were one of them, he couldn't do enough for you. On the other hand, if he thought you were stupid or lazy he could make life hell.'

'Was Paul Sutton one of his favourites?'

'Absolutely. For all his faults, Paul was the next best thing to a genius and Hockridge cultivated him assiduously. He used to give extra, unpaid supervisions. He even took Paul with him to a couple of foreign conventions. One was in New York and the other somewhere in Germany, I think.'

'So would you reckon it unlikely that Paul could have turned against his patron or given Hockridge some reason to show the other side of his nature?'

'Are you asking me, Nat, if I think Hockridge could have murdered his golden boy? Absolutely out of the question.'

'Yes, but,' Jenny lowered a forkful of spaghetti back to the plate, 'hell hath no fury like an old queen scorned.'

Sandra looked puzzled. 'Are you suggesting Hockridge was homosexual?'

Nat replied, 'It's a view we're coming round to. Do you disagree with it?'

Sandra shrugged. 'If he was that way inclined he certainly covered it up successfully.'

'Well, he would have had to back then, wouldn't he?' Jenny insisted.

The doctor laughed. 'Hey, we're only talking about ten years ago. It wasn't exactly the Dark Ages, you know. People tended to be fairly open about their sexuality.'

Jenny was persistent. 'Ah, but we're not talking about ten years ago, are we? At that time Hockridge was . . . what, early fifties? His basic attitudes were formed way, way back in his teenage years and then homosexuality was certainly taboo. Now,' Jenny leaned forward, warming to her subject, 'by the time he reached middle age he was a pretty confirmed misanthrope – right?'

Sandra nodded.

'Right. And what does misanthropy stem from?'

'You're the psychologist,' Sandra said.

'Unconscious self-loathing. I think Hockridge never came to terms with what he was, and that coloured all his relationships. They tended to be volatile. Now, if he formed a close attachment to Paul and then something went wrong between them, love would quickly turn to hate . . .'

Nat inclined his head. 'That's a working hypothesis. Let's try it from another angle. Sandra, what impression did you form of Sutton's sexuality?'

The doctor set down her knife and fork. She sat back, frowning with concentration for several seconds before replying. 'I think that was something that puzzled several of us at the time. If I attempt to answer that question it will inevitably be coloured by later experience. I would say that Paul Sutton loved himself so ardently that normal sexual emotion didn't get much of a look-in. He could have had several girls and probably he did but they were no more than casual one-nighters. What he enjoyed was power over other people. It amused him that he could make them *want* him whether or not he wanted them.'

'Was he bisexual?' Nat asked.

'Again, that's not quite the right question. I don't know whether he practised sodomy with anyone but I'm sure he wouldn't have hesitated if he thought he was going to gain something by it. Restrictions of all kinds – legal or moral – were irrelevant. He considered himself above them.'

Jenny looked at Nat. 'This is classic NPD. I've said that all along.'

'Would you agree with that?' Nat asked Sandra.

Again, she thought carefully before replying. 'Narcissistic Personality Disorder is very rare. Back in those days it was scarcely even recognized as a condition. But if Paul Sutton was to come into my surgery today I'd certainly recommend a psychiatric report and I wouldn't be surprised by an NPD diagnosis.' She sighed. 'But sometimes I wonder whether the old-fashioned explanations aren't best. That young man was just plain evil.'

Nat drained his glass. 'And that bring us, I suppose, to the $64,000 question: who do you think brought this devilish career to an abrupt end?'

Sandra shook her head. 'I'm no wiser than you on that score. I only had the newspaper reports to go on. I was interested enough to keep them.' She took a large manila envelope from her bag. 'You've probably been along to the *Evening Star* archive to see these, but if they're of any use to you please take them. They don't tell us very much. Back then I got the impression that everyone from the coroner downwards was concerned with keeping the story simple. It was a moral tale: this is what happens when students dabble in drugs. The fact that there was no sign of any disturbance or of anyone else having been in Paul's room made it easy for the police and everyone else – college, university, press – to point to Paul's death as a warning.'

'But you don't buy it?'

'No. It would have been totally out of character for Paul to shoot himself up with heroin.'

'But if someone else was involved, they'd have had to use a measure of force.'

'Or incapacitate him with drink,' Sandra suggested. 'The police found a couple of empty bottles of very good claret in the room and the contents of the stomach confirmed that Paul had swallowed a fair amount of it.'

'I suppose there was only one used glass.'

Sandra nodded.

Nat's brow creased in a frown of concentration. 'So, if we rule out suicide or accident, we're left with Sutton sitting in his room with someone he obviously knew. That someone watched him drink his way steadily through two bottles of wine, then calmly injected him with a syringe full of deadly narcotic. It doesn't sound very likely, does it?'

'The murderer could have tied his victim up and forced the booze down him,' Jenny suggested.

'No, that doesn't work,' Nat objected. 'There would have been signs of a struggle, wine splashed all over the place and rope marks on the victim's wrists.'

'OK.' Jenny tried again. 'How about this? Paul and one of his cronies do a private experiment to see what effects drugs and alcohol have on them. But Paul's companion is playing a different game. While he injects himself with a harmless substance, he provides Paul with something more lethal.'

Sandra looked dubious. 'It's the sort of bravado stunt Paul would have enjoyed but I still can't see him injecting himself. He knew what drugs could do and he despised people who used them.'

Nat sat back, eyes closed in concentration. He ran a finger along the bridge of his nose. Eventually he said, 'Drugs.'

The women looked at him expectantly.

Several more seconds passed before he went on. 'Are we sure that drugs are at the root of this business?' He looked from Jenny to Sandra and back again. When they made no comment, he said, 'I mean could trafficking in illegal substances account for the money Sutton apparently had? By all accounts he enjoyed an extraordinarily affluent life-style for a student. It must have cost him thousands a year. A little dealing among friends couldn't have supplied him with all the funds he needed to cut a dash . . . could it?'

Sandra pondered the question. 'Drugs were more expensive back then. A shot of heroin would have cost five times what it does now. Today the market's become so flooded that kids can turn themselves into zombies for the loose change in their pockets. I know; I run a rehab clinic. But ten years ago? Well, there were quite a few wealthy young-sters in Cambridge and Paul certainly cultivated them. He got himself invited to their country homes and foreign villas. He was desperate to be one of them. Spoiled kids with more money than sense attracted him like magnets.

But I can't really answer your question, Nat, because I don't know how the traffic worked back then.'

By this time they had reached the coffee stage and the three of them sat for a while in silence.

Eventually, Sandra said, 'I haven't been much help, have I? There's not enough evidence to get an old case reopened.'

'But you'd like to see it reopened?' Nat asked.

'I suppose what I'd really like is for someone to prove to me that Paul Sutton's death really was accidental. He wasn't a great loss to the world. I suppose the chances are he'd have gone from bad to worse. But we have to be optimistic. We have to believe that no one is beyond redemption. At least, I do. So it's outrageous that someone should have decided to deny him the chance to grow up, to mature, to put his massive talent to some good purpose.'

'With NPD, which is incurable, the chances are he'd have ended up in an institution,' Jenny said.

'Well, we shall never know, shall we?'

A sudden buzzing sound made Nat thrust a hand into a jacket pocket. 'Sorry about this,' he muttered as he put the mobile phone to his ear. He stumbled his way to the door, avoiding glares from the restaurant's few other customers. Outside the air was needle sharp.

'Who's that?' he asked.

'Tom Strang here, Dr Gye, duty porter. Sorry to disturb you but I tried your home number and Mrs Gye said to see if your mobile was switched on.'

'That's OK, Tom. What's so desperately important that it can't wait till tomorrow?'

'Well, Doctor, someone left a letter for you here at the porters' lodge and it's got URGENT across it in big capitals. I thought I ought to let you know.'

'How very odd. As it happens, I shall be coming back through town a bit later on. I'll pick it up then. Sorry you've been put to this trouble.'

'That's OK, Doctor. See you in a bit, then.'

Back inside, the women were already being helped into

their coats. Nat settled the bill. Ten minutes later, having escorted Sandra back to her hotel, he and Jenny set out on the short drive back to Cambridge. By the time he had dropped his passenger and taken a diversion back into the city centre the streets were deserted. As he parked on the double yellow line outside Beaufort the chapel clock struck eleven. In the porters' lodge, Strang sat comfortably behind his glass screen, engrossed in a paperback novel.

'Ah, there you are, Doctor. Chilly night to be out, isn't it? I popped the letter in your pigeon-hole.'

Nat found a plain white envelope with his name typed on it and the word URGENT in well-spaced red letters.

'Who delivered this?' Nat asked.

'Don't know, Doctor. It was left on the counter about half past seven while I was doing my rounds.'

Nat stuffed the letter in his overcoat pocket, bade the porter goodnight and climbed back behind the steering wheel.

He reached home to find some of the downstairs lights on but the house in silence. When he peered in through the bedroom door and called out quietly to Kathryn, the only response was a steady, deep breathing.

Only when he had settled himself on the sofa with a small brandy did he open the mysterious letter. It was computer-printed on copy paper and its message was succinct.

> Dr Gye, If you wish to avoid CERTAIN DISASTER for yourself AND your family you will inform Sir Joseph Zuylestein WITHIN 48 HOURS that you are abandoning your interference in the affairs of St Thomas's College. This is not an idle threat.

Nat finished his drink and went to bed. Sleep was a long time coming.

The Tenth Day of Christmas

It was after breakfast the following day that Nat showed the note to Kathryn. They were sitting in the study and he explained how he had come by the threat. Kathryn was indignant. She dropped the single sheet of paper on the desk.

'Melodramatic nutcase!' she muttered. 'What are you going to do about it?'

'I've been thinking about that most of the night. I must obviously do what the writer demands. Then, just to be on the safe side, I'm going to pack you and the boys off to London. Can you give them a treat – a bit of sightseeing, Madame Tussaud's, a panto perhaps? You know the sort of thing they like.'

Kathryn frowned. 'There are two problems with that. The first is that the office flat is booked. We've got a couple of designers over from New York Group HQ.'

'Book into a hotel for a few days. The boys will enjoy that. It'll make them feel very grown up. What's the second problem?'

'I can't believe you're just going to cave in. Whoever wrote this note must be very worried and that means you're getting close to the truth.'

'In that case he knows more than I do. The St Tom's business is a bloody, tangled mess at the moment for all that I can see.'

'So, let's go through it together. Let's see if I can help.' She paused. 'You always used to discuss these things with me.'

Nat refused to rise to the challenge. 'That's not the point, Darling. There's no way I'm going to risk the lives of my nearest and dearest just to dig old Zuylestein out of a hole.'

Kathryn picked up the letter. 'You really think this nutter is serious?'

'Well, I'm not playing poker with you and the boys for chips.'

She was absorbed in the note. 'The more I read this, the less convincing it seems. It's someone trying to sound menacing and not making a very good job of it. I mean "CERTAIN DISASTER". It's . . . I don't know . . . pompous, Victorian. Certainly not the kind of threat you'd expect from a hardened criminal.'

'Agreed, but if we assume that it was written by whoever is at the bottom of the St Tom's business then he's probably already killed once. He thinks he's got away with it all these years but now he's facing exposure and prison. He'll certainly kill again to avoid that.'

'Well, if he's that desperate why doesn't he just go ahead and kidnap one of us? Then he could hold us to ransom until he was sure you'd abandoned the case.'

'I think there are a couple of reasons for that. First of all, kidnapping requires organization. He'd need at least one other person to help him and a place to hide the victim away. The more complicated a plot gets, the greater the risk of something going wrong. And, then, once he'd released the victim he'd have no way of knowing that I'd stick to my side of the deal. Anyway, a simple threat is more effective. It plays on my fear. I don't know who this bastard is and whether he has the means to carry out his threat but I can't risk it and he knows that.'

'But,' Kathryn insisted, 'you do know who he is. At least you must have been able to whittle it down to a few possible suspects. So, come on, what have you discovered?'

'Well, if we're talking about people close to Sutton who might have had a motive to get rid of him, there's the dodgy lawyer, Tyrone. He's keeping information back and he's very keen to find out exactly what we know. Hockridge was top of the suspect list but obviously we can rule him out now. I bumped into Simeon Grimm a few days ago in St Tom's. He will have guessed why I was there and the chances are that he told the other fellows. Of the others who were here ten years ago and are still around now, there are three who could be suspect. I don't know much about them and, of course, I can't investigate them now.'

'Hmm!' Kathryn was thoughtful. 'What about Barny?'

'What do you mean?'

'Does anyone know that he's involved with your enquiries?'

'Tyrone knows.'

'Yes, but I mean anyone at St Tom's.'

'I don't think so.'

'Perhaps he could do some sniffing.'

'I've already asked him and I'm not going to press him further. That might put him at risk.'

'Still, at least you've got forty-eight hours to unmask the villain.'

'What do you mean?' Nat raised his voice. 'I've already told you I'm packing it in. I never wanted to get involved in the first place. This letter gives me a perfect out.'

'But you can't show it to Zuylestein.'

'Why ever not?'

'Just think what that would do to the poor man. How could he run a college knowing that one of his senior colleagues is a murderer? You'd have made things ten times worse for him than they were before.'

'Are you seriously suggesting that I ignore this threat to you and our children just to make life easier for the Master of St Thomas's?'

'I'm suggesting that you take full advantage of the dead-line the murderer has offered. You've got forty-eight hours to unmask him.'

'Less than thirty-six now.'

'Whatever.'

'Out of the question! There's no way—'

Kathryn interrupted, a puzzled frown on her face. 'Why do you suppose he gave you forty-eight hours? I mean, it takes away some of the urgency, doesn't it? Why not twenty-four hours? Why not, "Go and see Zuylestein straight away"?'

Intrigued despite himself, Nat pondered the question. 'Because,' he said slowly, 'he has no way of checking till the day after tomorrow. He can't phone up the master and say, "Oh, by the way, Sir Joseph, has that busybody, Gye, stopped nosing around in college affairs?"'

'Of course not. That would draw attention to himself. But what's so special about the day after tomorrow?'

Nat shrugged. 'I don't know.' Then, suddenly, 'Yes I do! Of course, it's the Epiphany Feast!'

'What's that?'

'Major event of the college year. Sort of annual stock-taking. The College Visitor presides over a meeting of the governing body to review all the ups and downs of the past year. Then there's a special service in chapel before everyone resorts to the hall for a slap-up meal. Zuylestein, himself, told me that he wanted to be able to report to the meeting that the F5 business had finally been laid to rest.'

'So you've got till then to sort it out?'

'Yes, but . . .'

'Look, I'll do a deal with you.' Kathryn came and stood in front of his chair. 'I'll take Ed and Jerry off to London today while you do your damnedest to nail this bastard. Then you can come and join us for a few days. We could both do with a break.'

Nat opened his mouth to protest but Kathryn put a finger to his lips.

'And,' she said, 'we'll take time out to have that talk we both need to have.' There was the sound of a car on the drive and she crossed to the window. 'Here comes your Dr Watson. I must go and start getting the boys organized.'

Minutes later Barny was sitting in the chair Kathryn had

vacated. He reported on his talk with Professor Hockridge's widow.

'So you think she knows who killed Sutton?'

'Knows or suspects and is not keen for the culprit to be brought to book.'

'So who is she likely to be protecting? Have you had any further thoughts about that shortlist I gave you?'

Barny drew a slim notebook from his pocket. 'I have made a few phone calls and, for good measure, I persuaded a friend in the local council's legal department to run off a copy of the coroner's report. Alas, I think that my enquiries give us very little to go on.' He turned over a couple of pages. 'David Sanderson is your totally dedicated college man. Lives and breathes St Thomas's. Reliable rumour has it that he had hopes of the mastership last year.'

'According to Sandra Cowley he took an unhealthy interest in young ladies.'

'Well, if so, it certainly didn't blight his career. The only oblique connection I can find with our deceased young friend is that for several years Sanderson coached the college first eight, which means that he was close to Tyrone.'

'But if he allowed his sexual entanglements to influence his examination marking, as has been alleged, that would have laid him open to blackmail. I reckon he's a serious contender. Who else have we got?'

'Simeon Grimm is a very straight-laced, ultra-conservative, dedicated enemy of change, particularly where the undergraduates are concerned. He has consistently opposed every liberalization of college regulations. For example, he fought a long campaign against the admittance of women to St Thomas's. One of his more cynical observations is still remembered by collectors of donnish epigrams. He is supposed to have objected at one meeting of the government body, "The young gentlemen have the young ladies here all night. I can't imagine why they want them here all day as well." When the drug scare hit the university it was

143

Grimm who led the ensuing purge, not only in St Thomas's. He was a one-man "Clean up Cambridge" campaign.'

'Would "vigilante" be too strong a word?'

'Probably not. You are wondering whether he took the law into his own hands with Sutton?'

'If he had identified Sutton as the focus of the drug traffic in St Tom's he would, surely, have confronted him.'

'Yes, but *murder*? I imagine he would simply have handed the young man over to the police.'

'I suppose so.' Nat paused. 'Something else you said struck a chord. Hang on a minute.' He turned to the computer and brought up his journal notes. 'You said Grimm opposed the admittance of women to St Thomas's.'

'Vehemently, according to my sources. It seems he's never reconciled himself to the female presence.'

'Then, it may be significant that all the residents of F5 who were disturbed by possible supernatural manifestations were women – Sarah Belman, Rebecca Tan, Lydia Tasker.'

'You think he might have indulged in a long-running misogynistic vendetta?'

'He seems to be a man with an *idée fixe*. And he has access to all the college rooms. *And* he has staunchly resisted any investigation of possible psychic phenomena.'

'So it would be precipitate to eliminate him from the suspect list.' Barny turned over another page. 'Tristram Philigrew's connections with the undergraduate body seem to have been almost entirely professional. However, he was for several years the college's wine steward and he ran a wine club for junior members.'

'Yes,' Nat turned back from the computer screen. 'Now that's interesting. On the night he died, Paul Sutton drank a large amount of expensive claret, presumably with a visitor to his room. What else do we know about Philigrew?'

'The only definite connection I can find with Sutton is that he was patron of the PS Society.'

'The what?'

'Our modest young friend founded an exclusive dining club and called it the PS Society – using his own initials. As you know, it is conventional for such ad hoc groups to invite a senior member to be their Maecenas. For a dining club Philigrew was the obvious candidate.'

'No reason, then, for any animus between him and Sutton?'

'On the contrary; Sutton apparently went out of his way to cultivate the Philigrews. He was more than once a guest at their house.'

'Does that leave anyone else on the shortlist?'

'Roger Sumpter was the other name you gave me but I have discovered nothing pertinent about him. Apparently, he hated Hockridge like poison. So, incidentally, did Grimm. But that is not much to the point.' He closed the notebook and returned it to his pocket. 'Has any of this been of help?'

Nat sighed. 'I'm sure it would be if we had time to mull it over. It's like being given a jigsaw puzzle with too many pieces and no picture for reference. It's possible to solve it if you go about it methodically and are prepared to devote as long as it takes. But we have virtually no time left. Zuylestein wants it sorted out by the day after tomorrow . . . And so does someone else.'

Nat told Barny about the threatening note. 'I think you should distance yourself from the business, now. There's someone desperate and dangerous out there and I don't want to put you at risk.'

Barny avoided a response. 'What we need is some opportunity to interview our suspect.'

'That was never an option. Sir Joseph was determined to keep the investigation secret.'

Barny looked thoughtful. 'They'll all be at the Epiphany Feast.'

'How does that help us?'

'I shall be there, too.' Barny explained how Madge Hockridge had invited him. 'I'll do a bit of delicate sleuthing.'

145

Nat shook his head firmly. 'I can't agree to that, Barny.'

The old lawyer smiled. 'My dear boy, you'll forgive me for pointing out that I don't need your agreement. I want to get to the bottom of this as much as you do. "Justice" is an overworked word, so perhaps I should not claim to be its passionate advocate. You might prefer to identify my motivation as insatiable curiosity. Whatever it is, having gone so far I'd like to take this business as far as I can. It's something to do with the rightness of things.'

'The rightness of things.' The phrase stuck in Nat's mind long after his friend had gone. That *was* what it was all about. The search for truth was not mere intellectual activity to be taken up or abandoned on a whim. It had a moral dimension. That was why it was important to stumble through the mists of time and clamber over the barriers of half-truth, lies, and threats put in the way by people with things to hide. Barny could see that. So could Kathryn. Nothing for it, then, but to make a last all-out effort to go through the information he had assembled and try to make it yield a coherent pattern. Part of him insisted that it was an impossible task. There were too many unrelated fragments and, between them, large, blank areas of unknowing. Then the other part of him, the stubborn part, hit back with the Tennysonian truism that the human spirit was destined to 'follow knowledge like a sinking star beyond the utmost bound of human thought'.

He saw his family off in the Mercedes, made himself a sandwich lunch and then settled down in the quiet house to think. Feet up on the sofa, he began with the bundle of press cuttings supplied by Sandra Cowley.

STUDENT DEATH IN DRUGS TRAGEDY – the *Evening Star* had given the breaking story front-page treatment but it was clear they had been short on hard facts. Beyond naming Sutton and identifying the cause of death the newspaper could offer little to justify the bold-type subheads. The best the editor could do was refer readers to an inside page and the interview with a local JP lamenting the spread of hard drugs among town and gown.

Nat lay back on the cushions. Tying Sutton in to the narcotics trade still did not add up. He cudgelled his brains in an attempt to work out why he was unhappy with it. What evidence was there to connect the student with anything more than dabbling in drugs? His parents had found a small quantity of heroin in his room. Sandra had identified him as a small-scale supplier but knew no details. According to her he had tried to persuade her to obtain narcotics, on the mistaken assumption that medical students had easy access to such substances. But, surely, if he was involved with a major drug ring he would not need to try arranging his own suppliers.

'Of course!' Nat said out loud. 'Paul Sutton was a loner! The last thing he would do would be to get entangled with a criminal syndicate. That would have made him a minnow in a big pool. Intolerable for a man who had to be the biggest and brightest fish in his own chosen pond.'

The telephone rang. It went on ringing while Nat searched for the handset. At last he tracked it down in the kitchen.

'Hello!' he said hurriedly.

'Ah, Dr Gye, is that you?'

'Yes.'

'Oh good. Gerald Sutton here. I'm so glad I caught you. Am I disturbing you?'

'Not at all. What can I do for you?'

There was hesitation at the other end of the line. Then, 'I just thought you'd like to know that Jane passed away yesterday afternoon.'

'Gerald, I'm so sorry.' The words were conventional but Nat's sense of shock was genuine.

'Thanks, Dr Gye. She didn't suffer much. I think I told you she was in hospital. They did everything they could but she had another heart attack.'

'Gerald, how dreadful for you. Are you all right? Is there someone there with you?'

147

'I'm OK. Truth to tell, it's a bit of a relief. She hadn't had much of a life these last few years.'

Nat struggled to find words that didn't sound trite. 'I don't suppose there's anything I can do, but . . .'

'Well that's it. That's why I was phoning.' He paused. 'When I got back from the hospital, do you know the first thing I did? I went and cleared out Paul's room. I should have done it years ago but Jane would never hear of it. She wouldn't even let Mr Tyrone, the lawyer, look through Paul's papers – and he was trying to help us. Anyway, point is I came across one or two things that might be useful to you. I wonder if I could pop up to Cambridge with them.'

'Er . . . yes, certainly. When would you like to come?'

'Well, would tomorrow be all right?'

'Yes. . . Look, why don't we have some lunch together? I know a quiet pub near here where we could meet.'

'That's very kind of you, Dr Gye. Are you sure it's not too much trouble?'

'No trouble at all. I'll look forward to it.' Nat gave Gerald Sutton directions to the Lamb at Frettlingham. Afterwards, he heated a kettle and made himself fresh coffee. He felt very flat. Jane Sutton's death was a depressing irony. She had believed with every fibre of her being that her son was no junkie or drug-trafficker. And she had been right, or almost right. Of that Nat was now convinced. It seemed grossly unfair that she would never see her faith vindicated.

He opened his laptop on the kitchen table and went to the latest page of his journal. He typed in a question.

If Sutton was not earning enough from the modest distribution of drugs, how was he funding his extravagant lifestyle?

By leaching Hockridge, his indulgent lover, perhaps. This could have led to a falling out between them until Hockridge eventually snapped and . . . No, that doesn't work. Whoever *did* kill

148

Sutton is still very much alive and issuing threats to avoid being unmasked.

Nat sat back, eyes closed. He suddenly realized that Gerald Sutton had just said something significant. What was it? Something about Tyrone. Yes, that was it: the lawyer had tried to get access to Paul's papers.

Secrets. Secrets Sutton might have written down. That's what this business was all about. Poisonous, poisonous secrets. Secrets that could undermine reputations, destroy lives. Sutton had so far insinuated himself into people's lives that he had discovered things they would pay to keep under wraps. One of them had been driven to the ultimate crime because that was the only way to be sure the unsavoury truth would never be known. The only alternative would be to go on being bled by Sutton for ever and a day. The irony was that murder had not silenced the blackmailer. The stories of hauntings in F5 had kept the old tragedy alive. And Sutton's mother had preserved all his belongings, including, perhaps, incriminating papers. The murderer could never be safe as long as there was the possibility of damning information coming out.

What was also true was that without that information it would be impossible to identify the killer. Perhaps Gerald had discovered the unholy grail. The answer to that would not be known for twenty-four hours. Time was running out – fast.

Nat returned to the computer journal.

If not Hockridge – then Tyrone?

Tyrone: an ambitious lawyer married to his senior partner's daughter and successfully building his career. He unexpectedly comes across the Suttons and realizes they're determined to get their son's death re-investigated. He agrees to act for them in the hope of discovering and suppressing any incriminating evidence that might still be around. He comes to Cambridge to find out if we've turned up anything linked to him.

149

What is he hiding?

His close involvement with Sutton's nefarious activities. We know he lied about his close connection with Sutton. They were known as the apostles.

Tyrone as murderer?

Probably ruthless and calculating enough but what's the motive?

Anyway, unlikely to use heroin for the job. It might put police on to the St Tom's network.

Philigrew, then?

Known to have been very friendly with Sutton. Could have been the person drinking pricey claret with him. He reacted dramatically when the news of the undergrad's death was publicly announced.

Guilty conscience?

Not necessarily. It could have been simple shock. The man he'd been with a few hours before was suddenly no more.

Sanderson?

If the rumours were true he certainly had something to hide. Sexual peccadilloes are one thing. Fiddling exam results quite another. As a medic he knew all about drugs, how to administer them, lethal dosages, etc.

Put him top of the list, then?

For now.

What about Grimm?

All we have against him is character – a walking Puritan conscience; a man determined to root out evil. If he knew about Sutton's narcotic activities, he'd have come down on him with all the wrath of an avenging angel.

But, murder?

More likely to have got him sent down.

Probably easier said than done. Sutton was the shining white hope of St Tom's in his year; all set for a starred first. Hockridge would have stood up for him, as would other members of the fellowship.

What if they *dared* not discipline him? Supposing Grimm confronted Sutton and Sutton defied him – 'Take any action against me and I'll go straight to the press with what I know about certain senior members of your precious college'?

Interesting theory. With St Tom's reputation at stake Grimm might certainly think that ends justified means. But it's all speculation. We've no evidence against any of these people.

Nat sat back, staring blankly at the ceiling. Barny was right; the only way to test the theories was to confront the possible culprits. But it was far too risky to let the old lawyer do that – on his own.

Nat logged off, gathered up his cap and overcoat and went for a walk to clear his head.

Later that afternoon, when Barnaby Cox telephoned Madge Hockridge to arrange to collect her for the Epiphany Feast, she had some news for him.

'I've been clearing Jeremy's desk today,' she explained. 'Not a difficult job. Fortunately, he was an obsessively tidy man. Never threw anything away but had a place for everything and kept everything in its place. As soon as the weather turns drier I shall enjoy a great big bonfire.'

Barny was alarmed. 'You will keep a careful look out for anything pertinent to what we were discussing yesterday.'

There was a cackle of laughter at the other end of the line. 'No cache of love letters or signed confession has so far come to light. However, I did make one slightly odd discovery.'

'Really?'

'Yes, the desk is one of those massive Victorian roll-top things. Quite hideous. It has lots of drawers and pigeon-holes and, of course, the obligatory secret compartment. Why anyone should call these little hidey-holes "secret" I can't imagine. They're always in the same place. Any half-way intelligent burglar would locate it in an instant.'

'And what was in this unsecret secret place?' Barny tried to keep the eagerness out of his voice.

'A key.'

'A key?'

'Yes. A very uninteresting, oldish key with a long shank. The sort that fits doors and cupboards. It doesn't belong here. I've tried it in all the doors round the house.'

'How intriguing. Presumably it unlocks something in Jeremy's rooms at college.'

'That's the conclusion I've come to. What I thought is this: if we got to St Tom's a bit early for the Epiphany do we could have a nose around.'

'That's an excellent idea. What's the running order for Epiphany events?'

'They have their powwow in the afternoon and then adjourn to the chapel to tell the Almighty what good little boys they've been since they last reported to him. Then it's up to the Drawing Room for drinks at seven followed by dinner in Hall at seven forty-five. If we go to Jeremy's room while they're all at their devotions we'll have an hour or so to explore.'

'Fine. I'll pick you up about five thirty. I look forward to it.'

'So do I,' Madge said and Barny thought he detected a real degree of warmth in her voice.

The Eleventh Day of Christmas

When Nat drew the curtains on 5 January he looked out on a village green across which half-hearted flurries of wet snow were drifting. Some of the local children were optimistically trying to have a snowball fight. Their efforts were doomed; the precipition was too slushy. The compacted missiles were small globules of ice. Even as Nat watched, one of the girls fell to the ground with a scream, clutching at her cheek and moments later the combat was broken up by an irate mother.

Later, when he was settled in his study, going through the newspaper reports of Sutton's death and the subsequent inquest, he reflected that trying to reconstruct the last hours of the dead student was similar to trying to make snowballs from wet snow. The material was inadequate for the task. He set the press clippings aside and deflected his attention to college business. It was no good. He could not settle to anything else.

A mid-morning telephone call did not help.

A man's voice said, 'Can I speak to Kathryn Gye, please?'

'I'm afraid she's in London, today,' Nat replied. 'May I ask who's calling?'

'Oh.' There was a moment's hesitation. 'Is that Mr Gye?'

'This is Dr Gye. And you are?'

'It's Mike . . . Er, no, on second thoughts it doesn't matter. I'll try her mobile.' The anonymous caller rang off.

Nat immediately made a 1471 call only to be told by a mechanical voice, 'the caller withheld their number'. He glowered at the handset before slamming it back on its rest. 'Kathryn, what the hell is going on?' he muttered. 'What are you hiding?' Of course, he reasoned with himself, the call could mean nothing. Just a business contact. Yet, taken together with Kathryn's strange conduct of late, what was he to think? Was a marriage doomed when the parties began keeping secrets from each other? There was that word again – 'secrets'. How corrosive they were. What power they gave. What fear they engendered. Kathryn had promised to talk everything through when they met in London. He was determined to hold her to that, yet fearful of what she might have to say. Perhaps he should phone Kathryn's parents. He suspected they knew something. He looked at his watch. No good calling now; it was still the middle of the night in Pittsburgh. Middle of the night! Suddenly Nat remembered the call that Kathryn's father had put through a couple of days earlier. He must have been phoning at about three a.m. Eastern Standard Time. Damn! Damn! Damn! What was going on!

He was glad when the time came to leave for his meeting with Gerald Sutton.

When he walked into the Lamb he saw that his guest had already arrived and was seated at a table in the far corner. His first impression was one of shock. It seemed scarcely possible that Sutton could have changed so much in a single week. The man who stood up to shake hands seemed to have shrunk, shrivelled. His physical appearance had not changed but he seemed to have contracted within himself. It was as though the real Gerald Sutton, or what was left of him, was looking out through the eyes of another man.

'Very good of you to see me,' Sutton said with his usual apologetic demeanour.

'Not at all. I'm just sorry it's under such sad circumstances.'

Sutton shrugged. 'Well, least said . . . Let me get you a drink.'

When they had ordered their drinks and food, Sutton opened the briefcase beside him and took out a large manila envelope which he laid on the table. 'It's a wise man who

154

knows his own son,' he said. He raised his half-pint glass to his lips. 'A wise man . . . and I've been a fool.'

'Our children never work out the way we think they will.' Nat tried to find something comforting to say. 'Paul was a very remarkable young man in many respects.'

'Oh, yes.' Sutton nodded. 'I never realized how remarkable till now. Like I said on the phone I cleared Paul's room a couple of days ago. I went at it like a bull in a china shop. Pulled everything out – bed, furniture, photos, books, rugs – the lot. I dragged them out to the back and burned them. And do you know why?'

'It was probably a way of working off your grief.'

'Not grief, Dr Gye, not grief. Anger. That room had been like a brick wall between us for ten years. It came between Jane and me in every imaginable way. I just wanted to tear it down. Still, I mustn't burden you with my problems. All Paul's files and papers went on the bonfire. I think they were mostly to do with his studies but I didn't look at them closely. But these,' he tapped the envelope, 'these are different. I rolled back the carpet – I was determined to destroy that as well. In one corner it was loose and under it a floorboard wasn't fixed down proper. I found this in the space underneath. I've had a quick look through it. Most of the names don't mean anything to me but I can understand enough to realize what he was up to. I'm disgusted, Dr Gye. Disgusted and ashamed.'

Nat opened the envelope and took out a sheaf of papers and a notebook. Opening the latter he saw columns of figures. Most entries had names beside them which meant nothing to Nat. Others, however, almost leaped from the page – Sanderson, Hockridge, Philigrew. The papers were letters, handwritten notes and photographs. There could be no doubt about the significance of the cache.

'Thank you for bringing this,' Nat said. 'It can't have been easy for you. It looks really useful. I don't want to raise your hopes but this could help us to get to the truth of your son's death.'

'I just never realized, Dr Gye. Never realized. I thought it was just the drugs. Obviously it was much more. Much worse.'

The food arrived and for some time the two men ate in silence. Then Sutton put down his knife and fork and looked across the table with pleading eyes. 'What sort of a man would he have become, Dr Gye?'

It was not a question that could be answered and Sutton continued with scarcely a pause. 'I mean, you hear about rapists and serial killers and the like and you think, My God, how can such creatures exist? Were they ever normal or was there something wrong with their genetic make-up? Was there some point at which their parents should have recognized the way they were going and done something to stamp out what was taking control of them?'

'If we had answers to those questions,' Nat said, 'we'd be a healthier society. What I *do* know is that you mustn't blame yourself for the way Paul turned out.'

'It's good of you to say so, Dr Gye, but no parent can shrug off responsibility. You should see some of the kids who live around us. Uncontrollable. They break into cars, knock over old ladies for their purses, wander the streets in gangs, shouting obscenities. Are you going to tell me that's not the responsibility of their parents? Of course it is.'

Nat searched hard for words of reassurance. 'There are some young people – we see them here perhaps more often than you might think – who have to live in the fast lane. It doesn't occur to them to go at the same speed as everyone else. In fact they would think it foolish to do so. If you own a Ferrari you don't drive it like a Mondeo.'

'Are you saying that the same rules don't apply to the likes of Paul?'

'No, of course not. It is just that it might be more difficult for them to accept those limitations most of us don't question.'

'You mean they think they're better than everyone else?'

'In a word, yes, and, in some ways they are because they

have special gifts. It can be hard for them to learn how to control them. The strongest boy in the class knows he can beat up the others, so he is tempted to become the class bully. The bright undergraduate knows he can outsmart his contemporaries – perhaps even his seniors – and is tempted to take advantage of that fact.'

'Paul certainly thought he was a cut above everyone else – especially his parents. Let me tell you what happened the last time we saw him. We came up unannounced just a few days before his exams. We wanted it to be a surprise. We were planning to take him out for dinner, just to wish him well in his finals. When we arrived he had some friends with him. They were drinking – and doing drugs for all I know. I'll always remember his words of greeting. Not, "Hello, Mum and Dad, thanks for coming." It was, "What the hell are you doing here?" He went out of his way to humiliate us. He laughed at us in front of his mates and said wasn't it amazing how beautiful flowers could grow out of mud. We turned round and went straight home. I'd even carved a model of his precious car. Very detailed. Took me days. Probably the best thing I've ever done. Pathetic, isn't it? It went straight on the bonfire when we got home. Jane, of course, still couldn't believe any ill of him. She said he was highly strung and obviously worried about his exams. She had this shining image of her wonderful boy and she never let go of it right to the end. All I can remember is that his last words to us were words of utter contempt.'

'I'm so sorry, Gerald, but I repeat what I said a few minutes ago: you mustn't blame yourself. This isn't just an empty platitude. You see, as a psychologist I can assure you that Paul was almost certainly suffering from a clinical condition known as Narcissistic Personality Disorder. It takes its name from the Greek legend of Narcissus, a youth who fell in love with his own reflection in a fountain. Mercifully, it's very rare but those afflicted with it have extreme fantasies about their own importance. They need constant praise and go out of their way to gain it. Praise, in turn, feeds their distorted self-image, so they become caught up in a vicious circle from which there's no escape. My guess is that, if Paul was still alive, he'd have been institutionalized by now.'

Gerald looked thoughtful. 'So Paul's death . . .'

'Might actually have been for the best.' Nat sighed. 'It's a terrible thing to say but he and several other people have been spared a great deal of potential pain.'

'Thank you, Dr Gye. That's a comfort – a real comfort.' Sutton sat up straight in his chair, as though a burden had been physically lifted from his shoulders. 'Have you come to any conclusion about this ghost business?'

'There's nothing conclusive. There rarely is in these cases but I'm still exploring the events surrounding Professor Hockridge's death and, like Mr Micawber, I'm ever hopeful that something will turn up.'

When they said goodbye at the end of lunch, Sutton's spirits seemed to have revived slightly and Nat felt that he had actually been of some help to the distraught widower. He drove straight to Beaufort and, having settled himself on the sofa, began to read Paul Sutton's hidden cache.

As he did so his excitement steadily mounted. The notebook – what Jenny would probably call his 'little black book', although it was actually green – was a tidy statement of income and expenditure. Sutton had noted – meticulously it seemed – monies received from parents and his college scholarship but of much more interest were the payments from several dozen other individuals. Many related to events Sutton had arranged. He appeared to have been a one-man entertainment organization. There were SP dinners, SP punting excursions, one SP skiing trip, one SP freshers' champagne reception and an SP Henley lunch, from all of which Sutton had made a healthy profit.

More ominous entries were 'to supplying M' or 'H'. Nat guessed that these initials stood for 'marijuana' and 'heroin' respectively. There were only half a dozen entries under this category and sales per unit ranged from £20 to £120. This suggested what Nat had already conjectured – that Sutton had only been a small-time supplier of drugs. A more substantial source of income was represented by frequent payments from five individuals. Two of the names meant nothing to Nat. The others were Sanderson, Hockridge and Philigrew. Sanderson had apparently donated £100 a month to the Sutton lifestyle fund. Against each occurrence of this item of income was set a mensual expenditure of £25 to 'PT'. From Philigrew Sutton had extracted a modest £40 per month. But it was Hockridge who had been by far the most lucrative source of cash. His contributions had been irregular but substantial. The largest was £5,000. This equated to the purchase, a few days later, of Sutton's sports car. Other payments varied from £250 to £1,000.

It was while Nat was doing a quick mental addition of all these sums that he noticed a single entry at the bottom of a page that he had previously missed. It read, 'S. Cowley – £150'. Nat reflected that that would have been a great deal of money to a medical student ten years ago.

Nat got up and poured himself a brandy before starting on the sheaf of papers and photographs. He switched on the main light and drew the curtains. Then he sat at his desk and removed the elastic band which held the papers together. Most of them were notes written in Sutton's flamboyant hand. But there were three letters and a small cache of photographs. He looked at the pictures first. A man riding a bicycle along the Cam towpath was presumably Sanderson coaching the St Thomas's boat. The picture of an unclothed young woman in a provocative pose had been cut from a man's magazine and Sutton had written across it 'Emma Wayte-Jones doing a vacation job'. A slightly out-of-focus shot of two people in a passionate embrace bore the caption 'Jim and Sandra Cowley – Oh brother!' The collection included a photograph of Sutton sharing a bed with an older man, presumably Hockridge.

All the material in Sutton's hoard was revolting and Nat felt sullied just looking at it. To be poring over these records of guilty secrets years later was to be almost as bad as the psychotic who had collected them for his own gratification. But there was no alternative. Nat had to analyse the information they described as dispassionately as possible. He logged on to his journal and entered certain conclusions. He sat back and surveyed the lines on the screen. What confronted him was a short list of suspects. He realized that it proved nothing but it did reveal the people who had most cause to want Paul Sutton dead and who had the opportunity to kill him. Gradually the loose ends were coming together. What faced him now was a process of elimination.

Nat made some phone calls. The first was to Peter Tyrone. When the lawyer came on the line Nat wasted no time on preliminaries.

'Tell me about the *annus mirabilis*,' he said.

There was a gasp at the other end of the line, followed by several minutes of bluster but eventually Nat extracted the information he needed.

The next call would, he knew, be more difficult. It was a call he did not want to make but he had no choice. Sandra Cowley was in her surgery when he rang but phoned back half an hour later.

Nat said, 'Sandra, it's been very good of you to help us with this business at St Thomas's but I wonder . . . would I be right in suggesting that your real motive was discovering how much we know – or don't know?'

'That's an astute observation,' Sandra replied cautiously. 'And do you know something that would be of concern to me?'

'I suggest that Paul Sutton's hold over you had nothing to do with drugs.'

'And is this pure speculation on your part?'

'I'm afraid I have to tell you that some of Sutton's papers have come to light.'

A silence at the other end of the line stretched for several seconds and Nat wondered if Sandra had thrown the receiver down. Eventually she said, 'Oh my God. Oh well, I suppose it really doesn't matter now.' She paused. 'I had a half-brother whose name was Jim.'

'But he was something more, wasn't he?'

'Yes. Somehow Paul Sutton found out about us and threatened to tell my parents. It would have destroyed them.'

'And you had to prevent that at all costs.'

'That's right.'

'Is that a confession?'

'Confession of intent to commit murder, certainly. I actually thought out various ways the deed might be done. But it would seem that someone actually beat me to it.'

Nat thought for some moments in silence and it was Sandra who asked, 'What are you going to do with the papers?'

'Suppose I were to hand them over to the police?'

'You would cause a lot of embarrassment and heartache to no purpose.'

'The evidence against you is circumstantial but if a new investigation was launched . . .'

'It would discover that I was a hundred miles away from Cambridge when Paul Sutton died.'

'You can prove that?'

'I spent part of the Easter vacation in Morocco and came back with hepatitis. I was laid up for several months and had to take a year out from my course. I was severely jaundiced for several months. I ached all over and I was as weak as a kitten. Even if I'd been able to get myself to Cambridge I wouldn't have had the energy to deal with Paul Sutton. I'm sorry if that explodes your neat theory, Nat.'

'And I'm immensely relieved that it does. What about Jim?'

'Full-time training for the Olympics – mostly in California. So what are you going to do with your evidence?'

'I'll see that it's destroyed.'

'Is that a promise?'

'Absolutely. And if I get to the bottom of this business in the next few hours you and Jim can finally forget all about it.'

'A bit late for Jim, I'm afraid. He was working in the Sudan with one of the aid agencies a couple of years ago and got caught in a skirmish between rebels and government troops. At least, that's the official story.'

'I'm sorry to hear it. Is there someone else in your life, now?'

'No, not yet. One day, perhaps. Who knows? Well, goodbye, Dr Nathaniel Gye.'

'Goodbye, Dr Sandra Cowley. Do stay in touch.'

'Of course.' She hung up.

Nat returned to the computer screen and removed her name from the list. Now there remained only two. He reached for the telephone again. The call was taken by an extremely agitated Joseph Zuylestein.

'Gye? Thank God it's you. I've been trying to reach you, on and off, all day. There was no answer on your home and college lines and when I tried again at Beaufort a little while ago you were engaged. Have you any news? We're out of time!'

Nat answered calmly. 'I can tell you, Sir Joseph, that the college will not have any more difficulty from the Suttons or their lawyer.'

'But, that's amazing. That's wonderful!' The master's relief almost vibrated down the line. 'How did you manage . . .?'

'I did very little, Sir Joseph. Mrs Sutton has died, and her husband does not intend to pursue the matter any further.'

'Why that's marvellous . . . I'm . . . er . . . sorry, of course, to hear about Mrs Sutton. That family has had more than its fair share of tragedy . . .' The master's expression of sympathy quickly ran into the sand. 'That means that I can report the matter closed to the governing body tomorrow and tell them that we can conclude our negotiations with our major benefactor.'

'May I urge an element of caution, Sir Joseph? I think it might be unwise to draw the final line under this unhappy business so publicly at your meeting.'

'What do you mean? What we needed was to get Tyrone off our backs. Providence seems to have intervened on our behalf.'

'Matters are not quite that simple. You asked me to investigate and, against my better judgement, I did so. Unfortunately, one can never know what skeletons one might encounter when one opens long-locked cupboards. Some issues have emerged which must now be dealt with. They cannot be ignored.'

'Oh, I think you can safely leave matters in our hands now, Dr Gye.'

Nat was appalled by the man's complacency. Hamelin had been emptied of rats; the hired Pied Piper could now be dismissed. Trying to keep the bitter edge out of his voice, he said, 'My life and the lives of my wife and children have been threatened by a member of your college.'

A stunned silence greeted the announcement. Then Zuylestein blustered. Words like 'preposterous' and 'mistaken' jostled with each other. Eventually, in a more subdued tone, he asked, 'What do you intend doing about this threat?'

'One course of action – the obvious one – would be to go to the police.'

'But that would ruin everything!'

'Precisely. That is why I suggest an alternative.'

'Go ahead, Dr Gye. I'm listening.'

'If you will be so kind as to invite me to your Epiphany Feast that will give me the opportunity for a quiet word with one or two of your colleagues. Before we actually sit down to dinner, I hope to have answers to my few remaining questions. That being so, you could, if you wished, announce your new benefaction to the assembled fellows and guests in Hall. I'm sure that would make a dramatic impact.'

'But supposing you don't receive satisfactory answers to your questions?'

'That, Sir Joseph, is a risk we shall both have to share.'

Epiphany: The Twelfth Day of Christmas

On 6 January Nat woke with a splitting headache. He had worked on the St Thomas's business until well beyond midnight and it had been after two a.m. before he got to bed. Thereafter, he had slept fitfully, his head full of jostling scraps of information. Poring over newspapers, Paul Sutton's private dossier and facts gleaned from various conversations over the last few days, he had constructed a possible sequence of events for Paul Sutton's last few hours. It was not foolproof by any means. He would not know if it was correct until he confronted certain people with it. If they stubbornly denied it he would be unable to make good his promise to Zuylestein.

A couple of codeine and some strong coffee reduced the throbbing in his temples and by the time he reached his desk Nat felt slightly better equipped to face the challenges of the new day. His calendar announced in suitably Gothic script that today was the Feast of the Epiphany. From his childhood and youth in the vicarage he knew the religious significance of the date. It marked the manifestation (Greek *epiphaneia*) of Christ to the Gentiles, represented by the Magi, who, he recalled his father earnestly pointing out, were not kings, nor were there three of them. Nat hoped desperately that he would have something to 'show' on this Epiphany day.

He called Kathryn on her mobile.

'Hello, Darling.' She sounded bright.

'Hello, you. How are you getting on?'

'Famously. We did a panto last night and we're just about to head for the London Eye. What are things like at your end? Any more violent threats?'

Nat reported on Gerald Sutton's visit and the revelations from Paul Sutton's unpleasant archive.

'So, you've got a couple of clear suspects?' Kathryn said.

'Yes. I plan to confront them at St Tom's Epiphany Feast this evening.'

'Well, go carefully, Darling.'

'I can't imagine anyone pulling out a lethal weapon during our distinguished gathering. Oh, by the way, someone called Mike was trying to get in touch with you yesterday.'

'Mike who?'

'He was reticent about revealing his identity.'

'Oh, *that* Mike. He reached me later on my mobile.'

'So, who is he?'

Kathryn hesitated slightly. 'I'll tell you tomorrow. What time do you think you'll be here?'

'Some time in the afternoon. I'll call you when I'm leaving.'

'OK, Darling. Must dash. I've got two excited little boys tugging at my sleeve. Bye!'

After he had returned the phone to its pod Nat spent several long moments staring at it. He was beginning to dread tomorrow. Compared to his showdown with Kathryn the St Thomas's business seemed suddenly unimportant.

The phone rang.

'Nathaniel, dear boy, interesting developments.' Barny explained about the key. 'So, what do you think it's for?'

'It sounds as though Hockridge wanted to keep something from prying wifely eyes.' Nat described the cache of Sutton's papers which had turned up. 'There were definitely matters that the late professor wanted to keep secret. I hope you find the chest or cupboard or whatever it is that conceals evidence of Hockridge's involvement with Sutton. It could help to tie up some more loose ends. By the way, I've also wangled an invitation to this evening's feast.'

'Good, good. We can compare notes.'

It was just after seven p.m. that Nat, dinner-jacketed and gowned, walked into the Fellows' Drawing Room at St Thomas's. He had just accepted a glass of champagne from a salver borne by one of the college staff when the master hurried up to him.

'Dr Gye, have you any more news for me?'

'Not yet, Sir Joseph.' Nat glanced at his watch. 'But we still have just over half an hour.'

'Half an hour!' Zuylestein struggled to keep his voice down. 'I doubt my nerves will survive!'

Nat looked over the master's shoulder and saw a tall man with a shock of dark hair watching him, while keeping up a conversation with two ladies. 'Excuse me, Sir Joseph, I must mingle.'

As soon as Nat had detached himself from the master, the tall man edged his way towards him through the throng.

'Dr Gye, isn't it?' he said with a wary smile.

'Yes, and you are Professor Sanderson.'

The other man nodded. 'It's true what they say about you then? You are something of a sleuth.'

'There's nothing clever about my recognizing you. I've seen your photograph.'

Sanderson could not conceal his anxiety. 'Where?' he demanded.

'I don't think we have time for lots of questions. I assume Peter Tyrone urged you to have a word with me.'

Sanderson lowered his voice. 'Can we find a quieter spot?' He led the way to the far end of the room where few guests had yet penetrated. When they could talk more freely he said, 'Tell me what you know – or think you know.'

'I know that there is a St Thomas's man passionately devoted to his college. I know that ten years ago he allowed that passion to warp his judgement. He supplied anabolic steroids to the college first eight. As a result they had an *annus mirabilis*, going head of the river for only the second time in the college's history.'

'They were a bloody good crew,' Sanderson said.

'So, perhaps your over-zealousness was unnecessary.'

'Well, I paid heavily enough for it.'

'Because Peter Tyrone, your accomplice, told his friend, Paul Sutton, and he put the squeeze on you.'

'That's right. I'm afraid Tyrone chose his confidential friends badly.'

'Oh, I think you underestimate him. Tyrone was part of the scam. For every hundred pounds you paid Sutton, he pocketed twenty-five.'

Sanderson's eyes opened wide. 'No! I don't believe it!'

'I thought that would surprise you. It's a guilty secret Tyrone's been keeping for years. Apparently, he still hasn't had the guts to come clean.'

'My God, when I think of all the blood, sweat and tears I put into coaching that crew. It was bad enough that Tyrone took all the glory, but this . . .'

'Still, when you silenced Sutton that must have given Tyrone a real fright. He must have been afraid he'd be next.'

Sanderson scowled. 'What do you mean, when I silenced Sutton?'

'I mean, when you injected him with an armful of heroin.'

'What?' Sanderson snorted. 'You think I . . . Ridiculous!' He sneered. 'Ever heard of the Hippocratic Oath? Most people in my profession take it very seriously. It means that if I were called to the bedside of a dying Hitler, I'd do all in my power to save him. I was mad as hell with Sutton but he was getting to the end of his time here.'

'Received wisdom was that he'd stay on to do a doctorate. Anyway the drug issue wasn't the only thing he had over you, was it?'

'Meaning?'

'A little matter of attractive female undergraduates and rigged exam results.'

Sanderson glowered, teeth clenched, cheeks reddening. 'That was sheer, bloody, malicious student gossip. There wasn't a shred of truth in it.'

Nat was about to press the point when he spotted through the crowd a suddenly familiar face. 'Who's that chap over there – short, glasses, balding?' he asked.

Sanderson glanced in the direction Nat indicated. 'That's Tristram Philigrew, our Senior Tutor.'

'Damn!' Nat said under his breath. 'Damn, damn, damn!'

'Nathaniel, good evening.'

Nat turned to see Barny Cox beside him, with an elegant, bright-eyed companion.

Barny made the introductions. 'Nathaniel Gye, this is Madge Hockridge.'

'A real pleasure to meet you,' Nat said and introduced Barny to Sanderson.

Somewhere a gong sounded. The professor muttered, 'Dinner; I must find my guests,' and drifted away.

'So, how did the treasure hunt go?' Nat asked.

'A complete flop!' Madge announced. 'We tried every drawer, box and cupboard in the room. There was no lock that our key came remotely near to fitting. I'm afraid I've wasted Barny's time.'

'Not at all, my dear, not at all. It was rather fun.'

The guests began moving towards the door. Nat saw Zuylestein looking towards him with an appealing look on his face. He gave a slight shake of the head and the master turned, shoulders drooping. Nat also noticed that Philigrew was holding back. He excused himself and crossed the room.

'Dr Philigrew, I believe. Perhaps I don't need to introduce myself.'

'No, indeed, Dr Gye.' Philigrew stared back through thick-lensed glasses, his face expressionless.

'Thank you for your letter,' Nat said, steadfastly retaining eye contact. He detected a slight raising of the eyebrows.

'Why are you interfering in St Thomas's business?' Philigrew demanded.

'Strange as it may seem, I'm trying to rescue the college from under a pile of suspicion, sordid rumour and crime.'

'There are things better left undisturbed.'

'But you and I both know that the past is not going to go away. It's been haunting this place – perhaps literally – for ten years. I suggest the time has come to face up to it.'

Philigrew looked around, as though seeking some escape route. At last he said, with all trace of belligerence gone from his voice, 'I am not prepared to go to prison for a crime I did not commit.'

'How about going to prison for threatening behaviour?'

'You could never prove I wrote that letter.'

Nat struggled to control his frustration. 'Can we stop this fencing? I've no desire to cause you any distress. Quite the reverse. I don't know whether you intended to carry out your threat against my family but I do know that you must be a desperately worried man even to contemplate it. All I want is to know what happened between you and Sutton.'

'What will you do with the information?'

'Let's try another approach. I'll tell you what I think happened all those years ago and you correct me if I'm wrong.'

Philigrew nodded and applied a handkerchief to the perspiration standing out on his head.

'You had a sexual relationship with Paul Sutton. He managed to take a compromising photograph of the two of you. I have seen that photograph but it's only this evening that I've realized that you were the "other man". I thought it was . . . someone else. Sutton used it to blackmail you and when you could stand it no more, you decided to kill him. You went to his room and spent a couple of hours plying him with strong drink. When he was insensible you emptied a syringeful of heroin into him. By the next morning he was dead. When the news was announced to the college you were seen to be very shaken. In fact, you collapsed.'

Philigrew emitted a long sigh. It was like a balloon deflating. 'Now you see why I have kept silent all this time. That sequence of events is exactly what any prosecuting counsel would advance and what any jury would readily believe. It is wrong in three vital particulars. For a start I am *not* homosexual and I was *not* having an affair with one of our own students. Secondly, the photograph you refer to is a fake.'

'Oh, come now. . .'

'It's true. I swear it. Sutton was a very keen photographer. He always had a camera with him. He loved dabbling in trick photographs. It is not difficult, I believe, for a clever amateur to superimpose images – in this case images of himself and me which, as you delicately put it, were "compromising". His intention was, as you rightly deduce, blackmail.'

He paused, then went on, 'We get some very strange people coming up to study here, as you will well know, but never, thank God, have I met anyone remotely like Paul Sutton. He was an utterly unscrupulous libertine for whom law, morality, common decency and friendship meant absolutely nothing. He was bent on experiencing everything and denying himself nothing. That comes expensive, hence his determination to extract money from everyone who came anywhere near him. I was very far from being the only one to be ensnared by his vicious greed.'

'No, indeed. There were many who had good cause to see Paul Sutton dead.'

'Yes, it was as much for their sake as my own that I decided to rid the world of him.'

'But, you said . . .'

Philigrew held up a hand. 'Hear me out and I will expose the third flaw in your reasoning. You want the full, sordid truth and you shall have it. My plan was a simple one. Sutton had tricked others into parting with what they could ill afford to lose. Very well, I would trick him into parting with life. I took some bottles of particularly good premier cru claret to his rooms on the pretence of asking his opinion. The conceited little sybarite fancied himself quite a connoisseur. My plan was to persuade him to try the delights of heroin – I knew he was on the fringe of the Cambridge drug scene. If I could get him to self-inject with a dose he believed to be safe my mission would be accomplished. Unfortunately, he wasn't having any. When it came to self-preservation his antennae were hyper-sensitive.'

Nat watched the last guests make their way from the room. 'So what happened?' he asked.

'I went on pouring good quality Bordeaux down his uneducated gullet until he was fairly insensible Then I pre-pared the syringe to inject a lethal dose. (Don't ask me how I came by the drug because I shan't tell you.) I'd just rolled his sleeve up when there was a knock at the door. I barely had time to disappear behind the curtains before someone came in.'

'Who was it?'

'I rather think it must have been my guardian angel. I heard him muttering but couldn't recognize the voice. Whoever it was stayed for about ten minutes while I sweated with my back to the window. As soon as the coast was clear I re-emerged. All I wanted to do was pick up the syringe which I'd left on the table and beat a retreat. To my astonishment I saw the syringe on the floor beside the slumped figure of Sutton and there was a mark on his arm. I couldn't believe my luck. All I had to do was wipe the bottles and the syringe clean of my fingerprints, remove my wine glass and put the syringe into Sutton's hand. That, Dr Gye, is the truth – and you know as well as I do that there isn't a jury in the land that would believe it. Are you going to put that to the test?'

Nat shook his head wearily. 'If we can't identify the real murderer, then, I suppose . . .' He shrugged. 'Hadn't we better go down to dinner?'

The two men crossed the room in silence. In the doorway Philigrew stopped. 'There was one other thing. Wait there a moment. I'll go and fetch it. My room is just along here.' He strode quickly along the corridor.

Nat waited on the landing, resting his back against the banister and staring straight ahead at the blank door of a cleaners' cupboard. Suddenly a thought flashed into his mind. He went back into the Fellows' Drawing Room. He turned right and looked at the cupboard containing old, unread books. Then he stepped back on to the landing, making some quick mental calculations.

'Here we are!' Philigrew returned. 'When I saw Sutton lying there and knew that he would die if he received no medical attention, this was on his lap.' He produced a small object from beneath his gown and placed it in Nat's hands. 'I don't know why I picked it up. Perhaps I felt that if it was the murderer's calling card he deserved to get away with his crime.'

In an instant Nat understood.

When they reached the Hall the guests were already seated and waiters were busy with plates and bottles of wine. Nat realized he had forgotten to consult the seating plan. But he had something else to do first. He sought out Barny and, bending down, said quietly, 'Do you have that key?'

Barny produced the object from his pocket and Nat hurried away with it. Back on the landing of G staircase he inserted it in the lock of what he had taken for a broom cupboard. It turned easily and the door opened to reveal a small space about a metre square. It was empty – except for a ladder.

He attracted little attention as he returned to the Hall, walked around high table, and had a quiet, whispered conversation with the master. Anyone remotely curious would have assumed that Nat was simply apologizing for his late arrival. But that would not have explained the look of intense relief that came over Sir Joseph's face.

Ghosts of Christmas Past

Travelling to London the next afternoon to rendezvous with his family, Nat detoured via Watford. It added at least an hour to his journey time but it had to be done. He had to report to Gerald Sutton that he now knew the identity of his son's killer. He also needed to work the St Thomas's business out of his own system. The previous evening Sir Joseph Zuylestein's little speech at the end of the feast had been rapturously received. He had announced the imminent reception of a large benefaction and had briefly outlined the uses to which the college proposed to put it. He had made no direct reference to the Sutton affair and its aftermath but members of the governing body and others in the know well understood what the master meant when he referred to certain 'difficulties' which had now been 'satisfactorily resolved'. After the meal Zuylestein had taken Nat aside to bestow effusive gratitude but for Nat there could be no indulging in warm self-satisfaction. He had returned to the empty house at Great Maddisham in maudlin mood, thinking only of ruined lives, guilty secrets and the burdens that had weighed people down for the past decade.

He felt no better now as he turned the car into the Suttons' suburban road and managed to find a parking space some fifty yards from the house. As he approached the front door it opened and Gerald Sutton emerged.

'Why, Dr Gye,' he exclaimed, 'what a surprise.'

'Sorry to call without warning but there have been certain developments since we last met and, as I was coming in this direction anyway . . . However, if you're busy.'

'Not at all, Dr Gye, not at all. Just a bit of shopping. Life goes on. Please . . .' He opened the door wide. He followed Nat into the lounge. 'Now . . . er . . . tea, coffee?'

'No thanks, I mustn't stay long.'

'Of course. Of course. You must be a very busy man, what with balancing two careers – university and TV. Anyway, do sit down.'

When they were seated opposite each other in deep armchairs, Nat surveyed the older man. What could he read in those eyes? Weariness? Apprehension? No, they seemed to be alive with eagerness. Hope, perhaps? Slowly he took something from his overcoat pocket and laid it on the coffee table between them.

Gerald Sutton stared at the beautifully crafted wooden model of a sports car and smiled. 'Thank God,' he breathed. 'Thank God. I could never understand how that disappeared. I suppose you know it all, now.'

'Pretty much, though I don't understand why you told me you'd burned this.'

'No, it was the other one I burned. This is what you might call the Mark II model. It was like this: when Jane and I visited Paul and got snubbed for our pains I was right angry. I did go straight out to the garden and made a bonfire and . . . Eventually I calmed down and decided to give Paul yet another last chance. Face him man to man. Tell him we'd forgiven him. That we still . . . you know . . . loved him. I knocked up another model, a token . . .'

'And you went to see him by yourself, unannounced?'

'It was my responsibility. I was his father. I couldn't just shrug off my part in the way he'd turned out, could I?' He looked imploringly at Nat. 'I thought we could talk. Huh! Fat chance! Do you know what I found? My precious son in a stupor from drink and drugs. There were bottles and glasses and a hypodermic syringe on the table and him lolling in the chair senseless. I tried to wake him but . . . I

176

thought to myself, Bloody hell, Gerald, is this what you've sired – this utter waste of space? I saw his sleeve was rolled up where he'd been injecting himself. I was so angry.' Gerald sighed deeply. 'I suppose I just flipped. I remember saying to Paul, "OK, if that's the way you want it, let's finish the job." I emptied the syringe into him. I didn't know what the effect would be and at that moment I didn't care. I suppose it must have occurred to me that he might die. That was probably why I left this with him.' He pointed to the model.

'A sort of visiting card?'

Gerald nodded. 'I never intended to get away with it, you see. I thought the police would be sure to trace the model back to me and then I'd confess. But they never did and I never had the guts to . . . I suppose if I had made a clean breast of it I'd have been in and out of prison by now.'

'Probably,' Nat agreed, 'but what you've suffered these last ten years has been worse than prison, hasn't it?'

'You can say that again. What with Jane's grief and the ghost business in Paul's room and Jane running a one-woman campaign to clear Paul's name, and Mr Tyrone promising to get at the truth . . . You're a shrink, Dr Gye, do you think I was subconsciously wanting to be discovered?'

Nat tried to reply with gravitas. He wanted to give this broken man something to live for. 'Gerald, you are basically a good man. I think you committed a crime that was so alien to your nature that your unconscious rebelled. As a result your mind has been a battleground ever since. But now the battle's over. You have to make peace with yourself. You asked me the other day what sort of a man Paul would have grown into. In all honesty I have to say the signs weren't good. You looked at those papers of his. You knew something about the lives he was ruining. Well, most of his victims were released by his death. Now, it's time for you to release yourself.'

'Easier said than done,' Gerald muttered with a shake of the head.

After a melancholy pause, Nat tried another tack. 'I wanted to ask you why you were so keen for me to investigate but I think I already know the answer.'

Gerald sank back in the armchair. Almost it seemed to Nat that the man was being absorbed, swallowed by the upholstery. 'I was sure you'd get to the bottom of it. I'd never have had the bottle to go to the police and say, "I murdered my own son." I came close to doing it a couple of times – when things got unbearable here – but . . . It wasn't that I was afraid for myself. Please believe that.' He stared intently, pleading to be understood.

'You must have been terrified to imagine what the truth would do to Jane.'

'That's it, Dr Gye. That's it exactly . . . Then your TV people phoned and . . . it seemed a godsend, an easy way out.' He paused, looking down at the model car still clenched tightly in his hands. 'Still, it's a mercy Jane never had to know.'

Nat looked at the broken man opposite. 'If it's any comfort, Gerald, there was part of me that didn't want to get to the truth. More than once I nearly gave up. I thought it was just because I didn't want to become personally involved but I realize now that I was trying to avoid the sheer tragedy of it all. I'm so sorry for what you've been through.'

'Oh, no, Dr Gye. It's me as should be saying sorry. I've been using you to do something I'm too much of a coward to do myself. So, what happens now?'

'As far as I'm concerned nothing. I don't believe in concealing a crime but in this case I can't see that there's anyone living who can possibly benefit from the truth coming out. So, I shan't go to the police unless you ask me to. And I urge you to think long and hard before taking any such decision. Have a holiday. Try to recover the years the locust has eaten. And now I must be on my way.' He stood abruptly. All that needed to be said had been said.

At the door the two men shook hands. Then Gerald went back inside and returned with the model. 'Will you keep this for me, Dr Gye? It's the only proof of my crime. I'll think about what you said and if, one day, I phone you up you can take it to the police and tell them what you know.'

It was just over an hour later that Nat joined Kathryn and the boys in a West End restaurant.

'You look bushed,' Kathryn said as they sat at a table consulting the menu.

'I've had better days and the thought of term starting next week doesn't exactly thrill me.'

'Do we still have the threat of instant assassination hanging over us?' Kathryn's smile was sardonic.

'No, I've dealt with that gentleman but it was touch and go.' Nat gave a brief account of the events of the last couple of days.

'Well done, you,' Kathryn said.

'It really got me down at times. I'm afraid I've been a bit of a bear with a sore head. Sorry.'

Kathryn laid her hand on his. 'I've been distracted, too. Not much of a support, I'm afraid.' She paused. 'You haven't explained the business of Barny and the key. What was that all about?'

'Ah, yes, that was the key to mystery in more senses than one. Sutton kept incriminating evidence on all his victims as we know. He boasted to them that he had a secure hiding place that they would never discover. Everyone assumed that this was somewhere in his room on F staircase.'

'They knew he seldom went home?'

'Exactly, so where else could it be? No one wanted the damning evidence turning up after Sutton's death. My guess is that Sanderson and Philigrew both took whatever opportunities arose to search F5. When they found nothing they did their best to have the room closed, and they were sporadically successful. But Hockridge went one better. He found a way of getting into the room via the loft and the cupboard outside the Fellows' Drawing Room. I had dismissed that idea because there was no way he could have used the cupboard *inside* the drawing room. It was only while I was waiting around on the landing before the Epiphany Feast that I realized that the broom cupboard there backed on to the other cupboard. So, whenever the coast was clear and F5 empty, Hockridge could search at his leisure without arousing suspicion by frequently asking for the key. Hence the strange noises that gave rise to the ghost stories.'

'But, hang on, Hockridge would only try the secret entrance to F5 when it was untenanted. So what scared some of the occupants? Perhaps Sutton's troubled spirit really was haunting the place.'

Nat smiled. 'Well, we mustn't close our minds to that possibility but I incline to think that what susceptible undergraduates heard was Hockridge bumbling around in the attic, looking for Sutton's hiding place.'

'No wonder Hockridge was so against your friend Jenny and her crew being allowed to investigate.'

'Ah, mention of my friend Jenny reminds me.' Nat reached into an inner pocket and produced an embossed card which he laid on the table in front of his wife. Kathryn read.

Mr and Mrs Francis Collard
request the pleasure of the company of
Dr and Mrs Nathaniel Gye
at the marriage of their daughter
Jennifer Frances
to
James Theodore Appleton
on Saturday 10 March at 11 a.m.
at
St Saviour's Church, Sorrington
And afterwards at the Fox and Pheasant Hotel,
Sorrington

Kathryn looked up, slightly pink-cheeked. 'How nice.'
Nat raised an eyebrow. 'Is that all you have to say?'

'I . . . I didn't realize Jenny was engaged. I've never seen her wearing a ring.'

'I gather that she and her fiancé are too prudent for such extravagances. They're putting all their money into a deposit for a flat and not bothering with luxuries like engagement rings.'

'I see. And you knew all about this?'

'Yes.'

'You never said.'

'I suppose I could reply, "You never asked." However, for your information, and according to Jenny, young James is dark-haired, six foot two and, I quote, "drop-dead gorgeous". The two of them met in Cambridge. James is now a management trainee in a major engineering firm. Oh, and, by the way, he was the university's middleweight boxing champion. So, you see, I never stood a chance.' He smiled and added, 'Even if I'd sought one.'

Kathryn grinned sheepishly. 'I suppose you're expecting me to grovel.'

'No, just tell me about Mike and what you've been keeping from me for the last couple of weeks.'

'Mummy, can I tell him?' Nat and Kathryn suddenly realized that Jerry had been following their conversation closely.

'No!' Kathryn said sharply. 'Don't you dare breathe a word.'

Nat was confused. 'So the boys are in on it – whatever "it" is,' he said.

'Yes, they had to be. Nat, *please* don't press me. Hang on just a little bit longer and you'll understand everything.'

Nat glowered. 'I hate secrets.'

'I know, Darling, but if you can just bear with me till after dinner all will be explained.'

When they had finished their meal they hailed a taxi and after a short ride alighted in front of a block of 1930s flats.

'Who lives here?' Nat asked as they waited for the lift. 'Is it the mysterious Mike?'

'Wait and see,' was all that Kathryn would say.

On the second floor she rang the bell of number twenty-seven. When the door opened Kathryn's father and mother stood in the small hallway beyond, smiling at them.

'Hi, Nat, welcome,' they both said, almost in unison.

'Ted, Amy,' Nat exclaimed in surprise. 'I thought you were both . . .'

'Back in the States?' Mr Carmichael said. 'That's what you were meant to think. Anyway, come in.'

Nat found himself in a compact but well-proportioned unfurnished apartment.

'What do you think?' Ted asked, waving an arm.

'Very nice,' Nat said. 'Are you moving over here?'

'Hell, no. This isn't for us.'

Kathryn wandered over to one of the windows. 'You can't see it now but there's a lovely view over the park.'

'We had planned to have it all sorted out by Christmas,' Ted said, 'but I guess lawyers are the same both sides of the pond. They don't know the meaning of the word "hurry". That's why Kathryn's had to keep coming up to town over the last few days to tie everything up. And we had to change our travel plans. Anyway, here we are.' He held out a bunch of keys. 'Happy Christmas, Nat.'

Nat stared back speechless for several seconds. 'You mean this is . . . ours?' he asked eventually. 'But how . . . why?'

'You've always said you wished you had a base in town,' Amy said. 'Kathryn will inherit everything from us one day. We just thought, Why in heck wait? Why not have a good wodge of it now while you and the boys can really enjoy it?'

Kathryn came up and linked her arm through Nat's. 'So, Darling, what do you think?'

'I don't know. Very grateful, of course, but it's a big thing to take in all at once. Is this what all the secrecy's been about?'

'Yes, Darling, and that's all it's been about. By the way, Mike is the estate agent. When he called earlier in the week it was to arrange handing over the keys. He's young enough to be my toy boy – if I'd sought one.' She gave him a hug. 'So now who's blushing?'

Ted laughed. 'Hey, you two, cut out the canoodling. I don't know about everyone else, but I could do with a drink. I've already sussed out the local watering holes and I reckon the best is just around the corner. So, come on, everyone.' He shepherded his flock towards the door.

Later, when they were all ensconced in a nearby pub and the boys were initiating their grandparents into the mysteries of hand-held computer games, Kathryn raised the St Thomas's affair again.

'What will happen to Gerald Sutton?'

Nat sighed. 'I believe he's already paid for his crime. The last ten years have been worse for him than any prison sentence.'

'But what about the other business?'

'You mean Hockridge's death?'

'Yes, I'm completely confused about that. You reckon it was Hockridge himself who was inadvertently responsible for the hauntings' scare on F staircase?'

'That's right. The key proves it.'

'So who did he meet up with on the stairs? Was there really a ghost?'

'Well,' Nat said, 'I have a theory about that but I can't put it to the test till I can get certain people to agree to a little experiment.'

Another four days elapsed before Nat was able to assemble his audience in St Thomas's College. They came one afternoon with varying degrees of enthusiasm and reluctance – Jenny, Andy, Cynthia Fell, Barny and Madge. They crowded into the landing and college servants' room of F staircase and Nat took up his position perched on the third step of the upper flight.

He thanked everyone for coming. 'I shall only keep you a few minutes,' he explained, 'but I hope that between us

183

we can clear up a mystery. The trouble with mysteries and secrets is that they generate rumours and conspiracy theories. What we don't know and don't understand can, quite literally, ruin lives. So if we can shed some light, that will be to everyone's advantage. What I'd like us to do is re-enact what happened here on the night that there was a terrible tragedy. I know that's unpleasant for you all but, as I say, if we can find out what really *did* happen I hope that will remove the burden of the unknown, with all its unpleasantness. So, would those of you who were here that night please taken up the positions you were in just before Professor Hockridge arrived?'

Jenny, Andy and Little Cynth placed themselves around the landing. Barny and Madge, as mere spectators, retreated into the college servants' room.

'Good. Now, I'll take the professor's role.' Nat went to the bottom of the staircase, then climbed it again. 'Now, I spend a few moments talking to you. Where should I be standing?'

Jenny said, 'Just a little forward.'

'Like this?' Nat shuffled a few inches.

'And facing?'

'Well, me and Andy.'

'So, he more or less had his back to Cynthia?'

'Yes.'

'And, then, he turned to climb the staircase? Right, I think I'm getting the picture. Andy, would you mind swapping places with me? I want to get a clear view of what happened next.' Out of the corner of his eye Nat noticed Cynthia diffidently half raise a hand. He ignored her. 'So, Andy, if you'd just try to imitate the professor climbing the stairs . . .'

Not without some muttering, the young man stepped across the landing and climbed the second flight of stairs. All eyes were upon him. Just as he reached the bend Nat dashed after him. He grabbed the hood of Andy's anorak and tugged it sharply. With a yell Andy teetered. He held out his arms in an attempt to regain his balance. Then he fell backwards and Nat caught him.

184

'What the hell do you think you're doing?' Andy shook himself free. 'I'm not staying for any more of this nonsense.'

'Sorry about startling you like that. Please just hang around for a couple more minutes and we'll be through.'

Jenny had been staring at the little drama wide-eyed. Now she spoke. 'Yes, that's it! That's what I saw. The professor shot his arms out in front of him.'

'But not to ward something off,' Nat said. 'He was desperately trying to keep his balance.'

'Yes, but there was no one anywhere near him.'

'No,' Nat agreed. 'That's puzzling, isn't it?' He looked at Little Cynth. 'Cynthia, did you want to say something?'

She shrugged and looked down at her feet. 'No, it doesn't matter.'

Nat smiled encouragingly. 'Come on, Cynthia. All contributions gratefully received.'

'Well, it's nothing really . . .' The girl was embarrassed at being the focus of attention. 'You left out the argument.'

'There was an argument?' Nat tried not to sound too eager.

'Well, not an argument exactly. There were just . . . you know . . . words.'

'Between the professor and Jenny?'

'Oh no!' Cynthia looked quite shocked. 'It was between the professor and Andy. The professor was saying that our psychic research was nonsense. He was very unpleasant and Andy stood up for us. He told the professor where to get off. That's right, isn't it, Jenny?'

Jenny nodded.

Nat said, laughing, 'I don't suppose they actually came to blows.'

'Almost,' Cynthia replied breathlessly. 'I thought they were going to. Andy did push him.'

'You stupid, impressionable kid!' Andy snapped. 'It was nothing like that. No dramatic confrontation. I was just concerned the old fool was going to go blundering into my equipment.'

'You tried to restrain him?'

'Just told him to go carefully; that's all.'

'Very reasonable,' Nat agreed. He smiled affably. 'By the way, Andy, what's your dog's name?'

'What are you talking about? I don't have a dog.'

'Oh, I just wondered what you used this for.' From his overcoat pocket he withdrew a retractable dog lead.

Andy stared at it, wide-eyed. 'How the hell did you . . .?'

'Your partner, Vicky, was kind enough to let me borrow it.'

'She had no bloody right to interfere with my things!'

'I noticed it when we called at your flat a few days ago. It struck me as an odd thing to do to remove most of the leather lead and replace it with fishing line. I actually snagged my overcoat on the hook. Does this represent a novel kind of fishing?' Nat enquired blandly.

Rowsell glared but said nothing.

'Or is it an ingenious contraption designed to literally bring down an overbearing and arrogant professor? You hated Hockridge, didn't you? You were convinced he was deliberately trying to stop you getting your doctorate. Isn't that really why you were here that night in December? You knew the professor was coming and he was certain to make himself objectionable. With any luck the opportunity might present itself to do "the old fool" a mischief. Not kill him of course, just humiliate him. And things couldn't have worked out better. Hockridge plays right into your hands. He insists on blundering up the staircase. Your brief altercation is enough to fix this hook to his coat collar. In the dark no one notices the nylon line which you play out as he climbs the stairs. Then you let it go taut. A slight tug and the professor topples down while you reel in the line. Then, while the girls are frozen in shock, you kneel beside Hockridge's sprawled body – not to help the poor man, but to detach your hook.'

Andy turned abruptly. 'That's it. I've had it with this nonsense! I'm off!'

Nat thrust out a hand to restrain him but the young man shook it off.

It was Madge Hockridge who prevented his departure. She stepped forward and, with a cross-court backhand that would have drawn applause at Wimbledon, she smacked her knuckles across Rowsell's cheek, her rings drawing blood. Andy crashed into the wall, slithered sideways and collapsed down the stairs.

Nat ran down and crouched over the recumbent form. Andy was groaning and shaking his head. Before the accidental assassin came to completely Nat bound some of the fishing line round his wrists. Then he phoned for the police.

Half an hour later a fully recovered Andy Rowsell had been taken into custody shouting an impressive repertoire of obscenities as he was pushed into the police car. Nat and Jenny stood in the gateway of St Thomas's College.

'I can't help feeling a bit disappointed,' Jenny said.

'Disappointed with Andy?'

'No, disappointed that there was no paranormal activity in St Tom's, after all.'

'Oh, I don't know about that. Wouldn't you say that the malevolent spirit of Paul Sutton has brooded over this place for more than ten years? As the Bard says, "the evil that men do lives after them".'

'I guess so. Anyway,' Jenny said, brightening suddenly, 'good can sometimes come out of evil.' She pointed along Jesus Lane to where the figures of Barny Cox and Madge Hockridge were walking arm-in-arm.